How Frail the Vessel

Enjoy

Sue Eato

How Frail the Vessel

Sue Eaton

This collection first published in the United Kingdom in 2025

by Corona Books UK
www.coronabooks.com

"How Frail the Vessel" © Sue Eaton 2025
"Evie's Friend" © Sue Eaton 2025
"The Boyfriend" © Sue Eaton 2021, 2025

An earlier version of "The Boyfriend" was published
separately as an e-book in 2021

ISBN 978-1-9996579-7-0

This is a work of fiction.
The stories, all names, characters and incidents portrayed in
this book are fictitious. No identification with actual persons,
places, buildings and products is intended or should be
inferred.

Contents

Introduction

The human mind is complicated and fragile. Like an egg, if you apply pressure in one direction it will withstand the force. In another it will break into many pieces.

The study of behaviour is fascinating but not always easy to process. The brain is an organ the same as the heart, lungs or liver. It can have problems as they can. Physical changes due to illness are easy to see and sympathise with. Problems stemming from the brain can result in behavioural changes and these are not always easy for the lay person to understand.

I began writing the story "How Frail the Vessel" during Covid. The enforced solitude gave my mind time to meander through events in my life as yet another big birthday loomed. Some events inevitably coloured the story.

Janet's story is an amalgam of my own experiences. Craig, on the other hand, is an exploration in what a person might do if pushed far enough. The story as a whole is a knitting together of many threads from my life. Fortunately for all, the ending I have written is fiction.

"Evie's Friend" began life as a ghost story. I'm hopeless at writing ghost stories, probably because I analyse such phenomena too closely and come up with a scientific explanation. Anyway, I began "Evie's Friend" as an attempt at a ghost story with the ghost child becoming stronger as Evie faded, but the characters had other ideas and suggested postpartum psychosis. Postpartum psychosis is fascinating – terrifying but fascinating. What the human mind is capable of is beyond the belief of mere mortals. Not to be confused with post-natal depression or 'baby blues', the symptoms of postpartum psychosis include hallucinations, delusions, mania or depression and confusion. It is serious, very serious.

"The Boyfriend" has already been available for some time as an ebook only. It is a psychological crime story influenced by the actions of the baddie in a film I saw many years ago and thoroughly enjoyed. You may wonder about the state of my own mind when you read the story.

I have been asked on numerous occasions if I would publish it as a paperback, but it really isn't long enough to justify the process. So, dear friends, I have included it with the other two stories.

Horror? Yes. Monsters? No. Just human beings doing human things.

Do you know what's happening behind the closed doors in your street?

Sue Eaton
July 2025

How Frail the Vessel

The first time was a total accident. I just happened to be in the right place at the right time – or the wrong place at the wrong time, depending on your view of things.

I was an aspiring photographer with a day job that was a lot less interesting. My degree in journalism hadn't morphed into a decent job, and while working in one of the big supermarkets wasn't my idea of a career, I did need to pay the rent and eat. Once work was over, I spent as much of my spare time as I could trying to find the photograph. The one that would open the door to a glorious career with some big newspaper. The one that everyone would talk about, like the picture of that poor girl in Vietnam. In order to achieve this, I roamed the city streets at night with my camera.

I had spent a lot of money on the camera, more than I could really afford – despite it being second-hand. Pre-loved as they say today. I was lucky enough to fall on a Canon PowerShot Pro 70, the latest model with all the specs I needed for my little hobby. A workmate put me on to it, knowing I like photography – and it was barely a quarter of the price in the shops. I didn't ask why the chap was selling it.

I don't drink, I'm not particularly interested in socialising with either sex, and I have no other hobbies. It was money well spent as far as I was concerned. My idea was to photograph the underbelly of society in the raw, to capture nature in its primeval glory and make the world shudder at humanity's inhumanity to its own kind.

That may sound dangerous and it was, so I dressed the part and carried cigarettes, a bottle of voddie and, when I could get them, the odd joint to share, in order to defuse any impending trouble. The knife was well hidden. I wasn't going to ask for trouble but if it found me … ?

I wasn't seeking company. I wanted to take photographs without people knowing, in order to get a true picture, warts and all, so to speak. Of course, I was bound to bump into those who wanted to know what I was doing, and that's where the drink and ciggies came in.

As I prowled, I dreamt of creating an exhibition or compiling a book for the coffee tables of the elite. I would become rich and famous and there would be a home for the homeless funded by my success and bearing my name. I saw myself dressed to the nines in an expensive dinner jacket accepting the Pulitzer Prize and smiling at the cameras. I would thank my mum and extol my council estate background for giving me the incentive to rise above it.

To this end, I was roaming the streets behind the town centre one cold night when I spotted two figures lit by the glow of a fire set in an old bin among the rubbish strewn about in the alley. Their shadows were thrown by the flames and flickered on the wall behind them. The pair appeared to be arguing and as I crept closer, camera at the ready, one pushed the other with such force that he fell to the ground, banging his head hard against the kerb. There was a snap as the skull cracked like an overripe melon, followed by a nauseating squelch. I could hardly bare to think of what I might see should I move – not that I could. I stood petrified for a few seconds, but the tableau the couple made, *silhouetted by the firelight, was perfect: the prone figure with another looming over him and the elongated shadow on the wall behind overhanging all. It all looked very Nosferatu, so I took several shots. I didn't hang about to see what happened; it was none of my business.*

* * *

Other than checking the pictures on the small screen of my camera, I didn't look at them properly until the following evening. The incident had unnerved me, if the truth be told, so I had hurried home with the ridiculous idea that the police would be after me with numerous questions. I had no wish to come to their notice, and you don't always see where the CCTV is pointing. I had work the next day, so decided I was better off trying to get some shut-eye before the alarm signalled the start of a new grind. Not that I slept much.

Breakfast news told me that a body had been found by an early-morning dog walker in that very alley, so I was sort of thankful that I hadn't stopped to help. I'm not a nasty person, but not everyone understands my hobby and I suspect the police would have been particularly suspicious. I kept my head down at work, but by the time I got home I was beginning to feel the need to have a look at what I had captured. Daylight and triviality can obliterate the fears of the night. I made myself a coffee and a Pot Noodle, and set about uploading the photos to my computer. As the pictures from the previous evening filled the screen, I was beginning to feel quietly impressed with myself – then I came to the last few: those where one figure was towering over another prone on the ground in the firelight. The last one of them was simply remarkable. I enhanced the picture a little and stared at what I had created. I shuddered involuntarily, and I felt the prickle as the small hairs on the back of my neck stood on end. Carefully, so as not to drop the Pot Noodle and splash the keyboard, I placed the tub down on the table top, feeling for a safe place with shaking hands. I couldn't take my eyes from the picture. I daren't in case what I thought I saw vanished, and the photograph would become like any other I took of the underbelly of the city at night.

There was something else in the picture, something I had not seen or ever expected to see. There was something that would make my name if I dared to use it. Something that excited and intrigued me and changed the course of my life.

I

'How are we today, Mum?'

Janet didn't expect an answer, and nor did she get one. She crossed herself and straightened the statuette of Our Lady on the bedside table, before sitting down at her mother's bedside like the dutiful daughter she was. She pulled out some knitting and chatted about her day, barely even wondering anymore if her mother could hear her or understand what she was saying. She prattled on until a knock at the door interrupted the flow and one of the carers pushed it open and popped her head around.

'Afternoon, Mrs Fanshaw. It's teatime. Is your mother eating at all?'

Janet turned to look at the young woman who had spoken. She recognised her as the young work-experience student who really looked as if she should have still been at school. She must have weighed about as much as a half-starved mouse.

'No dear,' Janet replied, wondering if the workforce ever spoke to one another. The girl should have known how her mother was. 'She's on a drip on account of her being "end-of-life". We're just keeping her comfortable.' She spoke as if it was some sort of achievement, which in a way it was. 'She's 89, you know, and has had a hard life.'

The carer nodded. She looked scared to death.

'Worked here long, duck?' Janet asked as she folded her knitting around the needles and the child-woman shook her head vigorously. 'I thought not. You'll get used to it.' The expression on the child-woman's face showed that she never would.

Janet turned back to her mother. 'It's five o'clock, Mum, or thereabouts. I've got to go and get cracking. Craig's coming tonight – did I tell you? He's coming for his tea and he wants it by six because he has to go out again. But he's been asking after you. He hasn't forgotten you. He's so busy at work he can't come and visit when he likes.' She felt a bit nervous, as if she would be caught in the lie and crossed her fingers as she said that, but she knew her mother would like to hear it. In reality, there were times when she had to remind her son that he even had a grandmother and that she was at death's door and it would be nice if he went to visit her before it was too late.

She wasn't looking forward to the tea. Jim, her husband, would start needling his son as he usually did, and Craig would answer back and before she knew it all hell would break loose, and Craig would storm out and Jim would stride into the front room and slam the door and then she'd hear the telly at full blast while she'd be left with the debris of the tea table and a sink full of washing up.

'I'll be back later, Mum,' she said softly. 'End-of-life' meant that she could stay with her mother for as long as she pleased. An evening sitting beside her silent parent would be restful.

* * *

Craig followed his mother so closely through the back door that she wondered if he had been waiting outside for her return. He would know that his dad would be home alone while she was out.

'Hello, Mum. What's for tea?'

Janet smiled. Nothing changed. He had always used those very words when he came home from school of an evening. First the crash as the front door was flung open, then his coat, bag and shoes in an untidy heap on the hall floor, and finally he would sprint into the kitchen with his eye on the fridge and the customary greeting on his lips.

Craig could hear the television turned up loudly in the front room. He nodded in that direction. 'No change there, then.' It was a statement.

'He's finding retirement a bit hard. No structure, you see,' she explained to her son as she tucked her shopping bag between the washing machine and the fridge, before heading for the sink in order to wash her hands.

'He's just a moody bastard and well you know it,' Craig retorted, his head inside the fridge. He pulled out a bottle of milk. 'Fancy a coffee?'

'No thank you. I'm going to crack on with the tea. Where are you going tonight?' She turned on the oven as she waited for him to move away from the fridge.

'Just out.' He shook the kettle and, finding it had some water in, switched it on.

'Just out where?' She removed an already-prepared shepherd's pie from the fridge and a bag of frozen peas from the freezer below.

'Just meeting some mates.' He opened the coffee jar and spooned some into a mug he found on the draining board.

'Which mates? Anyone I know?' She stretched up to reach a saucepan from the rack and poured in some peas.

'No. When will tea be ready? Only I said I'd be there by half seven.'

'You need to find a nice girl. Settle down,' she said, rattling plates and cutlery. 'Some good news to cheer me up. We're already eight years into this new Millennium.'

Craig sighed. 'Where have you been, anyway? It's quite cold out there.'

'To visit your gran in the nursing home.'

'How's Gran?' he asked belatedly, as he poured the boiling water into the cup.

'She'd go happy if she knew you were settled – so don't change the subject,' his mother told him.

'I will when I'm good and ready. I don't earn enough at the moment, but I will – I will.' He splashed some milk into the coffee and stirred it.

'You should have had that promotion, you know. You've been there longer than that Gavin Snape – and he's years younger than you. Assistant manager at his age. I don't know what the world's coming to. Mind you, his mother's a pushy bugger.'

'Don't harp on, Mum. Dad'll start soon enough.'

'Happen you're right, but I'm only saying. I don't know what they'd do without you, I don't.'

* * *

Craig knew that they'd cope very well without him. He was on his last warning and he needed the job in order to keep his flat and food on the table. As it was, he ate at his mother's whenever he felt he could put up with his father. He did just enough to get by and now, just when he needed to up his act, something else had taken his fancy and his mind was not on his job.

'So, how is Gran?' he asked again. A thought had just occurred to him.

'So-so,' his mother told him, which told him nothing.

'How so-so?'

'Well, she's not got much longer. The home say I can visit when I like.'

'Are you okay there on your own?' Craig knew his dad wouldn't put himself out and go with her.

'It's quite restful sitting there. There's no expectations. I'm going back after tea. Stay the night. They've put a put-you-up next to her bed, but I don't know, not with my hip.'

'I could go some nights,' Craig said. 'It would save your joints. You look washed out.' He watched her put the shepherd's pie in the oven before placing the saucepan of peas on the hob.

'I don't know about that. You have shifts at the supermarket, don't you? It's open all night.'

'I can change shifts if I need. It's a family thing.'

'Back again when your money won't stretch from payday to payday?' Craig saw his mother jump at the sound of the voice. Neither had heard Jim open the door. He was a devious bastard.

'Hello dear, we've only just walked in,' Janet said a little too brightly.

'That Gavin Snape seems to be doing alright for hisself,' Jim provoked. Craig had a retort ready but bit his tongue. Instead, he kept quiet as it would only have started a row and he hadn't time for it; he had other things on his mind. Plus, he was hungry and his mum's shepherd's pie was so good he could put up with his father for an hour or so.

'Ever thought of helping your mother instead of sitting on your fat arse while she runs herself ragged cooking you tea and then going to see to her own mother. You could at least have set the table.' He eyed the pile of cutlery waiting to be placed.

Jim sat himself down in his usual chair and opened his paper. 'Is it ready yet?'

Janet prayed that her son wouldn't answer him back. She didn't feel she could face the resulting scrap.

'It won't be long, dear. Would you like a cup of tea while you're waiting?'

'I have a cup after I've eaten, as well you know,' he snapped.

The room descended into silence, and silence was something Janet found difficult to cope with. 'Craig's offered to go and sit with his gran. Save my hip,' she announced brightly.

''Bout bloody time,' the newspaper retorted.

Craig sat firm. He only had to last until the meal was over.

* * *

Janet and her son walked out together. 'Thanks for helping with the dishes. I did appreciate it. Take no notice of your dad. He's …'

'…finding retirement difficult. I know, you keep saying, but nothing I ever do is right. If I help, I'm after something; if I don't, I'm an idle bugger. I can't do right for doing wrong.'

Craig had learnt long ago to shut his mind off from his father's continued griping. The resulting rows only hurt his mother, who ended up picking up the pieces – sometimes literally. 'Will you let me sit with Gran?' he queried. 'It's too much for one person and you have your hip to think about. We could take it in turns.'

'I don't know. What if I'm not there when she needs me?'

'You'll have to see to Dad, whatever. You'll have to leave her then. I could take over at teatime and stay overnight. It'll help your hip.'

Janet smiled at her son. He wasn't so bad. 'Alright, if you insist. But you will ring me if anything changes – you know what I mean. I'm not looking forward to that put-you-up, but I don't like to think of her going on her own.' Janet's voice caught at the thought of her mother's passing. 'You think you're prepared, but I doubt I am.'

Walking the Streets

I've decided I need another picture, just to be sure, but I don't expect to stumble across another death any time soon. I suppose the only thing I can do is roam the streets and hope. Of course, I could make it happen – if you know what I mean. I feel sorry for the homeless. It could have been me if Mum hadn't stumped up for the flat. I'm more than willing to help where I can, but some of them don't want help. Rather get off their heads on heroin, which is lethal. Some of these poor bastards would be better off by helping me get the pictures I need than living the drug-raddled existence they do now.

Best to take a breath, youth. You don't want to do anything daft.

I know it's dangerous but I actually like being out at night. It's a different world. The noises are different, clearer somehow without the background chunter of daily living. You can distinguish the dog's yelp and the angry shout telling it to shut the fuck up. A single car goes by. I swear I could tell you the make if I was so inclined.

The air is clearer. You can taste the difference as you breathe it in. There are fewer exhaust fumes, no cloying perfume mingling with ciggy smoke, apart from my own that is – although I rarely smoke when I'm on a case. It's too likely to give me away. There's a lack of the sickening odour of street food to clench the gut and make you realise you only had one piece of toast for breakfast, and that without butter because you've spent your last penny on a packet of fags. Instead, you get the rotting garbage smell from the bins outside of the restaurants, because that's where I find most of my inspiration. I watch from the shadows while the homeless raid the food bins and argue over scraps and bones. Sometimes they get lucky and the restaurant owner will give them bags of leftovers.

I feel like a shadow as I move silently through the back streets of the city observing life in the night, life in the raw. Nobody knows I'm there so their behaviour is natural. I don't want them to pose or shy away. I think I'll call myself Shadow. When I open my exhibition I'll wear a black silk suit in a Japanese style. I will be masked. A black half-mask across my eyes and half of my face. I've always fancied one of those. I might just darken my hair a bit too. It's quite dark already but it will convey the image I want.

The walls and floor of my studio will be painted black, and the pictures will be stark black and white with just one thing coloured in some, like they do in arty films. Red is a good colour. It stands out, vibrant and strong. There will be up-lighting directed on the pictures and nothing much else.

I will be an enigma, and everyone will be talking about the nameless photographer who takes such rare and exquisite pictures that convey the hidden soul of those who call the streets home. I'll still do the coffee table book. It'll just be anonymous.

And only I will know who I really am.

II

Janet Fanshaw née Murfin had always wanted just two things in life. She wanted to be a primary school teacher and she wanted children. She loved school, the smell of polish and milk mingled with meat pie and cabbage. She enjoyed learning and proved to be intelligent. Her parents, workers in the local potbank, were thrilled with her ambitions. She was a late baby, born when they thought they'd never have children, and because she was their only child they felt that they would be able to fund her university education in order for her to fulfil her dreams.

Janet grew up cossetted and naïve, and didn't really understand the nuances of sex and procreation until she was well into her teens. She wasn't like some of the other girls who were always chattering about boys and weddings. She never envisaged the type of man she would marry. She just knew she needed one if she was to have her babies. She had no siblings but her friends at school had younger brothers and sisters and she would spend a lot of time with them. She played out with the other children in the neighbourhood and that was where she learnt all the lessons of life. How to smoke, what cheap vodka tasted like and the back-of-the-bike-shed facts of life, which was perhaps why Janet found herself pregnant at the age of seventeen.

James (Jimmy) Fanshaw was one of those obvious good-lookers, a know-it-all prat who girls with a sheltered upbringing like Janet fell for. The more street-wise knew to steer clear. She started dating him shortly after her seventeenth birthday and thought she'd had her three wishes in one. He was so good-looking with his permed curls that reminded her of the actor she had a crush on in *The Professionals*, a programme about special agents that she avidly watched on the television. She was a good-looking girl and the pair turned heads wherever they went. She was the envy of her friends.

Patricia, her cousin and best friend, was positively salivating. 'My tummy flips when I look at that gorgeous face,' she drooled. 'You must think you've died and gone to heaven.'

Initially Janet would have agreed with her, but as the weeks went by Jimmy became more insistent that he should be able to treat her as his own personal possession. He questioned her closely when he saw her talking to one of Patricia's older brothers and refused to believe that he was a cousin and she was only giving him a message to take to his mother. He liked her to dress provocatively but then become unhappy when she did so as he thought she was enticing other boys. It upset her to think she displeased him, so when he suggested she dropped her knickers for him she barely hesitated.

'Aren't you going to wear a thingy?' she whispered.

He stopped pawing her breast and glared at her. 'Jimmy Fanshaw does not wear anything he doesn't want. He's a brave boy. He goes commando,' he told her.

'I can't get pregnant,' she insisted.

'No you can't so don't even think about it.'

Janet was still ignorant about a lot of things, but by now she knew where babies came from and didn't think you could simply choose as to whether you got pregnant or not. There were things you wore or pills you took to prevent a pregnancy.

'Jimmy,' she whined.

'Do you still want to go out with me?' he asked, rubbing himself against her.

'Of course I do.'

'Then you'll please me,' he told her. 'Anyway, you can't get pregnant the first time. I should know.'

She didn't get pregnant that time so believed him when he said she couldn't if they did it standing up.

* * *

'Are you alright, our Janet?' Patricia asked. 'You look really pale. Have you just been sick?'

Janet nodded, wiping her mouth as she left the cubicle.

The girls were in the sixth-form toilets. They had just got to school and Janet had had a horrendous journey in, trying not to throw up on the bus the whole time.

'You know what that means!' Patricia laughed at her own joke, but instead of joining in Janet burst into tears.

'Oh, our Janet. You're not? Does Auntie Glad know?'

'I daren't tell Mum,' Janet mumbled. 'She's so proud of me for going to the university. It'll kill her.' She slid down the wall and sat on the floor sobbing.

'You can't stay here,' Patricia warned her.' Someone will come in, put two and two together, and as this is a grammar school will get four, and your mum'll know before lunchtime.'

'I can't have this baby,' Janet wailed.

'Get up, Janet. Wash your face and put on a brave one for now. We'll talk about this at home tonight.'

Janet was never sure how she got through the day. She felt constantly sick, and even the teachers commented on her pallor, thinking she was coming down with a tummy bug. She hadn't the courage to disabuse them.

* * *

'Ayup Janet. What's to do?' her Aunt Dorothy said as the girls walked into the kitchen. She took in Janet's swollen eyes and blotchy face. 'Had a row with your mum?'

Janet shook her head not feeling able to speak.

'You look dreadful. What's up? You haven't had an accident, have you? Does your mum know? Does she know you're here?'

Janet shook her head and her cousin sighed.

'She's just found out she's pregnant,' Patricia announced as she flopped onto the old settee they kept in their kitchen-cum-diner. She picked up a crumpled copy of *Jackie* as the silence pervaded the room. 'Well, she is.'

Patricia's mother took a long look at her niece. 'Eh our Janet. Who'd have thought it?' The girl burst into tears again. 'I take it your mother doesn't know?'

Janet shook her head.

Although Janet's Aunt Dorothy was the younger sister, she often seemed the older, and she was certainly more worldly wise than her sister Gladys. Dorothy had had her eldest, Patrick, barely six months after her wedding and just after her seventeenth birthday.

'Pat, go and fetch your Auntie Glad. I'll put the kettle on.'

'No, I can't tell her, not yet,' Janet cried.

'The sooner you tell your parents, the more choices you'll have, my girl,' Dorothy told her. 'Go on, our Pat.'

Janet hadn't thought about choices, other than perhaps she'd wake up and find it all a dream. She sat on the old settee after Pat had gone for her mother and considered what her aunt had said.

'How far along are you? Her Aunt Dorothy's voice startled her for a moment.

'Mmm, I've missed one period. The next was due a couple of days ago,' she whispered. She had been hoping she'd miscounted.

'Have you done a test?' Dorothy asked

'Test?'

'Yes, a test.'

'I thought I would see a doctor for a test.' Janet hadn't dared to take one because she knew that a positive result would make it real and until then she could always hope.

'Come on, our Janet, you know full well you can buy

them from the chemist,' Dorothy informed her. 'Do it yourself at home.'

Janet shook her head. How could she go into the local chemist and ask for a pregnancy testing kit? It would be all round the estate before she got home. She was so deep in thought she never heard the back door open.

'Ayup Dot. Janet? What are you doing here? Tea's nearly ready.' Gladys looked from her daughter to her sister. 'What's to do?'

'Go on, our Janet, tell her,' Dorothy said kindly as she passed Gladys a cup of tea.

* * *

Gladys felt her vision tunnel and she went so light-headed that she sat down heavily on the nearest kitchen chair with a thump, tea slopping in the saucer and splashing across the back of her hand. She knew her daughter and had known that something wasn't right for a week or so now. She had asked what the matter was, but only got a snarled 'I'm fine. Don't keep on,' in reply. She had presumed it was to do with that boy she was seeing and it seems she was right. She knew Janet had been sick a couple of times and had hoped it was just nerves with her mock exams looming, but it seemed not. 'No, our Janet, you can't be. You're going to the university. You've got it all planned.'

'Sorry Mum,' was all she could muster.

'Your dad'll go mad. He's been telling everyone how clever you are. That you'll go to the university once you've sat your A-levels.' The tears streamed silently down her face as she pulled her rosary out of her apron pocket. Janet couldn't bear to look at her.

* * *

Janet's dad didn't go outwardly mad as her mother predicted, but she could tell he was very, very angry. She had wanted to wait until he'd had his tea and then sit down and explain everything, but both she and her mother were that upset that he'd guessed something was up as soon as he'd walked in.

She felt him stop as if all bodily functions had ceased. No breath, no heartbeat, no blood coursing through his veins. Not able to digest what he had heard. Time itself had stopped. She waited for the fallout, but all he said was, 'The dirty little bastard. He'll marry you of course.' It sounded so final. No talk of options. He said nothing to her. He didn't even look at her, and she felt such pain she thought her heart had cracked.

'I'll have my tea, Mother, and then I'll go round and have a word with his dad. I happen to know he's on overtime tonight. We'll sort this.' With that he sat in his chair at the head of the table and picked up the evening paper while Gladys dished up the overcooked sausage and mash. Janet couldn't force a morsel through the lump in her throat but nor dare she leave the table. Albert Murfin was known to be a stubborn man who once his mind was made up would not change it even if Christ himself arranged the Second Coming just to ask him nicely if he would do so. Her options, as her Auntie Dot called them, would be whatever her father told her they would be.

* * *

Albert Murfin returned from Jimmy's home within an hour. 'We're to go to tea on Sunday to sort this out.' With that he went into the front room and Janet and her

26

mother heard him turn the television on. Neither dared to go in even when *Coronation Street* started.

* * *

Rene Fanshaw hoped that the Murfins would consider it bad manners to argue with anyone who had provided you with decent food and drink, and she had prepared a good spread – the perfect Sunday tea – in the hope that it would keep things civil. A hope shared by Gladys Murfin.

The meal was a short, largely silent affair. It had been agreed that they would eat first and then discuss the issues the two young people were facing. Rene's few attempts at starting polite conversation floundered, and only the occasional 'Another cup?' or 'Please help yourself to sandwiches,' interrupted the silence. Janet stared at the snowy white tablecloth laden with tinned salmon and cucumber sandwiches that she knew would only make her sick if she tried to eat them. Jimmy just sat there next to her with a sullen expression on his face.

They gave up, not even bothering with the Victoria sponge, and once the tea things were cleared away the arguing began.

'The way I see it, it takes two …' Len Fanshaw began.

'Now Len...' Rene started but was cut off by Bert.

'We had this out the other night. If you'd have told that boy "no" once in a while he'd have known the meaning of it,' Janet's father snapped.

Janet started to cry but no one seemed to notice.

'Don't take that tone. He knows right from wrong. He's been told,' Len huffed. 'You've spoilt that girl of yours. She can do no wrong …'

Gladys made a small moue but remained silent.

'She knows better than to open her legs to any Tom, Dick or Harry,' Bert snarled. The gasp around the table stopped any further language of that sort. 'She was coerced that's what she was,' he mumbled.

'My lad doesn't need to coerce anybody. He could have any girl he likes.'

'It's a pity he didn't take another, then.'

'Will you two stop this arguing? It's not doing any good,' Rene snapped. 'The damage is done and we need to resolve it in the best way we can.'

'Well, my girl's not one to do that sort of thing unless she was coerced; that's what I think,' Bert flustered. 'He's been swanking about like some girl with them curls. It were bound to end in tears.' Len opened his mouth but Bert held up his hand. 'Our Janet was going to the university. He's put a bloody stop to that. The least he can do is stand by her.'

Janet shuddered.

'But Bert,' Rene whined, her hand on her son's. 'There's no need for weddings today.'

'Don't start, Rene. I don't care what year it is; the child will be a bastard unless it has a name. Now – dates. It'll have to be soon, before she shows.'

The Passing

I missed one last night. I just wasn't in the right place at the right time. Not that I knew about it until this morning. It's started the day off very badly and now nothing will go right. It'll be hard to keep my cool with the idiots I work with. To pretend I find their stupid jokes funny. That their bullying is banter. The news item kept running and rerunning in my head until I swear I would have hit the next person who made some snide remark. Instead, I banged my mug so hard against the countertop I broke it right down the middle. The stares I got made me realise I needed to calm down. Be more Shadow.

When I sell my work as The Shadow I shall be able to afford a whole set of mugs. I might even run to cups and saucers. And posh glasses – different ones for different types of drink.

I must practise patience. The Shadow wouldn't show such emotion. The Shadow would appear cold and detached even if underneath he was seething. He would plan his revenge with icy precision, not crack a mug in temper. He would get himself back out there and slide through the shadows looking for the best compositions. Poke his bad luck right in the eye with the photo to die for.

I don't really wish that people would die, but let's face it it's a fact of life. Street life is hard, and fights are the daily norm from what I've seen.

The thing is, it is cold out there. Spring might well be on its way, but there was a frost last night, which was how I missed the photograph. I stopped by a group of old men who were sitting around a fire. They had some food they'd been given by the people who owned the nearby café. They do that when they shut instead of throwing it away. They had a bottle of cheap brandy as well, to keep out the cold. We got chatting and before I knew it, it was getting light and I needed some kip before work or else I'd get it in the neck from Snape.

It appeared the bundle of rags in the corner by the shop

door was a body, frozen to death while I sat talking.
    I will have to wait just a bit longer.

III

'Haven't you finished stacking those shelves yet, Fanshaw?'

Snape's supercilious voice grated into Craig's thoughts. He had been totally absorbed in his daydreams, but, to be fair, he could stack shelves in his sleep. Besides, he'd only been assigned the task a few minutes before. Snape was a bully. He knew Craig was an easy target who had pushed his luck with management once too often. He was now on his last warning so wouldn't dare answer back. Besides, Snape's early promotion had gone straight to his head, and Craig wasn't the only one he made life difficult for.

'I'll have to get the work experience youth to show you how it's done,' Snape continued, after checking there were no shoppers close enough to hear him.

Craig itched to punch the arrogant smirk from his line-manager's face but instead he carried on stacking the tins of dog food, one on top of another, pointedly ensuring that the labels faced the front. He'd had enough practice with his father of ignoring snide remarks.

'I asked you a question,' Snape smarted. 'Have the decency to answer.'

'No, Mr Snape, sir.' Craig spoke without turning. 'As you are well aware, I was only assigned this task …' he made a show of looking at his watch, '…15 minutes ago, sir. I doubt even the work experience lad could have finished in that time, sir.'

Snape was about to retort when a couple rounded the end of the aisle and began choosing pet food.

'Well, get a move on, I've a list of things that need doing before the end of your shift.'

As the manager turned to leave the loudspeaker burst into life.

'A member of the sanitation team is needed in Aisle 7. Aisle 7.'

Snape spun on his heel. The couple had made their choice and were well out of the way. 'Fanshaw! Go and see what's happened in Aisle 7.'

'I'm not a member of the sanitation team.'

'Tough.' Snape stepped into Craig's personal space. 'I happen to know you're on your final warning,' he smirked. Craig stepped back as his line manager leant forward. 'I'm not convinced your grandmother died – again. I'd do as I was told if I was you.'

Craig opened his mouth to speak but decided that the more he tried to explain the truth the more it would sound as if he was trying to convince himself, never mind his boss. He was careful with his excuses, prided himself in keeping on top of the ones he'd used. The trouble was he couldn't boast about it without giving his game away. Besides, his grandmother really had died.

'You'll be after time off for the funeral next,' Snape continued.

'Whatever you say,' Craig said aloud with a muttered 'Mein Fuhrer' as Snape turned to leave. Fortunately, a customer caught the manager's attention and the remark was left in the air.

Craig deliberately left the pallet of dog food in the centre of the aisle and rather than asking for a call out on the intercom made his way to the staff area, slamming open the door. He looked around to see only one other person in the room.

'Where's Gill?' he asked Adrian, his colleague who was slouched in a chair with a mug of coffee in his hand.

'In the loo having a hot flush.'

'What about Debbie?'

'In with her, fanning her with the *Daily Mirror*.'

'Snape wants some mess cleaning up...'

'Fanshaw.' Snape had made his way into the staff area. 'Sorted that mess in Aisle 7 yet?'

Adrian put his mug on the table and stared at the pair.

'You'd better hurry up,' Snape continued. 'Your shift finishes in a few minutes and you've still got to finish stacking the dog food, and I do believe the cat food's getting low.' He suddenly noticed he had an audience. 'Break over, Buckley. Onward and upward, onward and upward.' With that he swept out, snapping the door shut behind him.

'I don't know how you can let Snape get away with speaking to you like that. I'd complain,' Adrian observed as he crossed the room to place his mug on the counter above the dishwasher, '...or hit him in the chops.'

'I'm hardly flavour of the month,' Craig sighed. 'I daren't antagonise him or I'll be out on my ear and he knows it. I really need the money. I already owe last month's rent.'

'My brother, Ross, has started work at the hospital,' Adrian told him. 'They're looking for staff.'

'What sort of staff? I don't know anything about medicine.'

'He's a porter and I know they're after more. I'd give it

32

a go, mate, if I were you. Hang on a minute, I'll get him to call you with the details. Can I give him your number?'

'Yeah, no probs.'

Adrian whisked out his phone and tapped out the message. 'There you are, easy peasy. He should get in touch with you.'

'Thanks, Ade. You're a mate. But what happens when I want a reference? Snape's not likely to give me a good'un is he?'

'Use Billy.'

'Billy's not my line-manager, though. Snape is.'

'Billy won't care. He gives the same reference for everyone who asks. I don't think he knows half of them. Just do it – good luck.'

* * *

Craig was so incensed with Snape's behaviour that he left the pallet of dog food where it was and, grabbing his coat, he left the supermarket one minute before his official clocking-off time.

A message from Adrian's brother came through shortly after he got home. He opened his computer and found the application form. Three cups of coffee, two hours and one Pot Noodle later, Craig was ready to give up but the thought of more Snape encouraged him to keep on until it was finished. There were a few days before the form had to be submitted, so he decided to leave it until the next day, reread it and then send it. It would give him time to speak to Billy as well.

It was quite late and he was on the morning shift in the supermarket but decided he would give himself a treat before bed.

No One Messes with The Shadow

I am The Shadow.

Whatever The Shadow puts up with during his daily life does not affect him as he goes about his nightly crusade. He sucks it up and uses the energy it creates to fulfil his ambitions.

I am patiently awaiting the day when The Shadow opens his first exhibition here in his home town. It will coincide with the town's 900th year celebrations. Everyone will be there, television, newspaper reporters, a minor royal ... no, not a minor royal, the Queen. The Queen will be there. She'll be honoured to open it.

Tickets will be invitation only and I'll make sure Snape has one. Printed on parchment, trimmed in gold leaf, the wording on the invitation in perfect calligraphy.

I shall wait behind the scenes until everyone is there, milling around the studio with crystal flutes of champagne, nibbling on exquisite amuse-bouche. Between bites they'll be eagerly discussing who this unknown marvel is. Does anyone know?

I shall choose the precise moment to glide out and drift among the crowd, as silent as the Shadow I am. I'll eavesdrop on the comments, basking in the glow of the compliments.

I shall slowly circle the room and come up behind Snape and whisper in his ear before melting into the darker reaches of the room.

He'll spin round, mouth agape, looking to see who spoke to him. Trying to understand what was said and why.

I will take the greatest of pleasure in the look on that

face. It will be as satisfying as a slap but won't bring me down to his level.

I am above other men. I am The Shadow.

IV

'Eh our Janet, you've done your mother proud,' Patricia reflected as she surveyed the food set out in The Waggon and Horses after her aunt's funeral. 'Although I'd have thought you'd have had it at the Sports Club by the crem. It's a bit more up market there.'

'Well I did think about it, but Jim drinks here and they do do a good spread. Plus there's not many of us, is there?'

'Aye, well, Jim isn't so good at keeping friends,' Pat agreed.

'Besides,' Janet continued, 'Pauline the landlady's been really kind since Mum died – helping with …' She paused and glanced across at her husband. 'Helping, you know.'

Her cousin did know. 'Aye, well …' Patricia looked across the room to where Jim was sitting drinking steadily.

Janet followed her gaze. 'He's finding retirement difficult. No structure,' she told her cousin. Patricia just sniffed and then noticed another family member she'd not spoken to since the last funeral and excused herself. Janet sighed and looked around the room, but the few guests were chatting in groups. There was no one standing alone waiting to be included and no one seemed to be seeking her out. She'd been well out of the loop since her mother took ill. Actually, Jim hadn't wanted her in any loop for so long it had been her and Craig for quite a while. People were wary of speaking to her as they knew how Jim would react when he'd had a few.

Janet was not wrong about one thing: Jim's retirement hadn't helped. He'd never been one for a hobby, unless you counted darts and dominoes in the Working Men's Club. He'd stopped that after some misunderstanding with the committee, so apart from drinking in The Waggon and Horses he spent most of his time in front of the television. He didn't like it if Janet went out for anything other than essential shopping, but she did stand her ground where her mother had been concerned. It had cost her but at least she could sleep at night; she'd not let her mother down. She was glad that Craig had left home. That had cost her too and not just the rent money, but it meant less arguments at home, so it was worth it in the long run.

She looked around for her son. She hadn't seen him for a while. He was probably outside smoking. She wished he wouldn't, but he was an adult so there wasn't much she could do about it. Her attention was taken by Patricia's youngest lad, Kyle, who was standing beside Jim and gesticulating to gain someone's attention. Young Bethany, Pat's eldest granddaughter, was standing to one side, pale and crying over something. Kyle's father was moving rapidly across the room to join him while Patricia was heading for her.

'Janet,' she whispered theatrically so that everyone could hear, 'can't you do something about that husband of yours? He's bloody drunk as per and making a right nuisance of hisself.'

Janet sighed. She had been afraid that that would happen, but had hoped it would have taken longer. She was on the verge of tears. It was her mother's funeral, and he couldn't even give her that time. Where was Craig? She couldn't sort this out on her own. She was exhausted.

Pat grabbed at her cousin's shoulder. 'He's leering at our Bethany. Pawing at her.' She craned her neck. 'Oh, her mother's there now. Janet, you'll have to do something. She's only fourteen. There's a right row brewing.'

'Have you seen our Craig?' she asked Patricia.

'I don't know why you don't just leave him. He's never been no good and you know it.'

'Leave it, Pat, will you? Just for today. I'll sort it.'

But Pat wouldn't leave it. 'You should never have married him. I don't know what Uncle Bert were thinking.'

Janet stopped her. 'Where's Craig?'

'It's a crying shame for that lad. And you. You don't need this today of all days. Now look – some people are already getting their coats. Steve?' She called across the room to her husband. 'Go find Craig and then help get his father home. You and Kyle.' She turned to Janet who looked ready to burst into tears. 'I'll stay with Janet. Get her a cup of tea. Go on then, you lummox.' She waved him away.

Patricia guided Janet to a seat in a small alcove where she was shielded from the other guests, albeit there were only one or two left and that was only because they were nosy and wanted to see how things panned out.

'I'll go get you a cup of tea. Eh, Janet, what's to do?'

With that, Janet did burst into tears. *Eh, Janet, what's to do?* It could have been her mother talking. Patricia patted her arm and went towards the bar.

37

She was still dabbing her eyes when her cousin returned with a mug of tea and a glass. 'Get that down you. Pauline's sent you a brandy chaser. Want to talk?'

Janet did but not in public. She would rather wait until she got home. Jim would sleep it off and she and Patricia could put the world to rights.

'I know what it's like. How I felt after my mum died,' Patricia urged. 'What's with Jim? And don't tell me any nonsense about not getting on with retirement. I know what he's like. I used to listen to your mother talking to mine when they thought I was out of the way making tea in the kitchen. Broke her heart, some of the gossip she heard about Jim. It did, I can tell you. Well?'

'If you'll let me get a word in, I might,' Janet sniffed. She had always been able to talk to her mother, but now she was gone. Gladys had been opposed to the wedding along with Rene, but the men, as old-fashioned as they were, had won out. There had been no need for marriage; it had been the late nineteen seventies not the early sixties. That was when her Aunty Dorothy had fallen pregnant with Patrick, Patricia's oldest brother. It would have been acceptable for Janet to have had the child and then gone back to school. Her mother was willing to look after it.

As it turned out there was no baby, not then anyway. Jim had insisted on poached salmon for the reception meal while knowing full well Janet hadn't been able to eat fish since she got pregnant. He made her try some as well. Said it would make her look ungrateful if she didn't. She managed to style it out at first, but just the few morsels she had ingested upset her so much she had to rush from the table to throw up. The reaction was so violent and she was so racked with pain that she didn't realise at first that she was losing the baby. It was just too ironical.

Her Aunt Dorothy and Pat wanted her to leave Jim and get a divorce, but she was a good Catholic girl and felt, rightly or wrongly, that it was a penance for getting pregnant and spoiling her parents' expectations of her. Janet was as stubborn as her father. She was a married woman. She had said her vows before God and she was going to stick with them regardless of what the rest of the family thought. Her father was proud of her for that and that's what kept her going.

It wasn't the last baby she would lose. It seemed she was prone to a condition called clinical spontaneous abortion. After two more miscarriages, Craig was like a gift from heaven. They didn't try again, so he remained an only one. Perhaps she did spoil him. Jim thought she did and voiced it on many occasions.

'Well?' Pat insisted, breaking into her thoughts.

'Give me a minute, will you? Let me drink this tea.'

She was further saved from talking by Kyle returning after dropping the others off. He dropped his car keys on the table and headed for the bar. His mother opened her mouth, but he pre-empted her. 'Hang slack, Mum. Let me get a drink.'

'You're driving, aren't you?'

'One won't hurt,' he called. 'I need it after that little fracas.'

* * *

Kyle sat down at the table with the two ladies. 'Eh, Aunty Janet. I've left him with Dad and Craig. He's in a right two and eight. Best stay here for a bit.'

'What happened?' Janet wasn't really sure she wanted

39

to know but would need to in order to deal with her husband when she got home.

'Well, all I did was walk in. I'd been out for a smoke. I saw him with Bethany. He was ever so close, leaning over her and she looked like she was getting upset, but no one else seemed to notice. I went up to them to see what was what and he started on me. Telling me I shouldn't be here – that he didn't know why I was invited. I tried to reason with him, but I thought he was going to hit me.'

'Eh, our Kyle! He never?' his mother cried.

'I am sorry, Kyle,' Janet apologised. 'It's the drink talking, you know. I'd better go and sort him out.' She knew what he was like around the young lasses. She'd tried to laugh it off more than once and pretend it was all in fun, but she'd seen the looks the others gave and the way the young girls – and girls they were – kept away from him. She was glad she'd had a boy. Even so, she'd had her work cut out keeping him from more than one beating for some minor misdemeanour.

'You just sit there,' Patricia told her. 'I'll get you another cup of tea. You're not going home on your own.'

'You stay there, Aunty Janet. He'll be alright, Craig and Dad are there,' Kyle reminded them.

'Janet, you'll go and grab some night things and then come to us. It's Aunty Glad's – your mother's – funeral. You can stay at ours tonight and have a bit of pampering. We'll take you home in the morning and see what's what. No questions – just do it.'

Janet just nodded. Patricia had always taken the lead when they were younger. She was just a couple of months older, but people could be forgiven for thinking it was more like years.

Everyone had gone home now that the excitement was over, and the lounge was deserted. Tears threatened again.

Pastures New

The Shadow is on the move. It's one thing taking a mundane job in order to fund the photography but every man has his pride. The Shadow takes no shit from no man – or woman.

I've packed in my old job and got another. I didn't hand my notice in until I was certain. This one will suit me much better. You may think I'm very lucky, jobs being scarce, but this is at the hospital. They need all the help they can get. Not everyone can stomach some of the things they see there. Accidents, fights, all sorts of injures. They don't always stay the course. I've not taken a position of responsibility, though. I need all my faculties for my work as The Shadow. It's just a means to an end, rent and food, that sort of stuff.

I'm used to shift work as the supermarket was 24/7. I'll still be able to roam the city on my nights off and have access to seriously ill people while at work. Result. My experiment can go ahead at twice the pace.

I didn't tell anyone about me applying until I heard I'd got the job. I made it sound like it was a doddle. The money's better too, so I bought some cakes and we made it a little celebration, Mum and me. Dad said I wouldn't last five minutes as it would be real work. I made the mistake of answering him back and we ended up having a row and I walked out. Mum was crying. I was cross with myself afterwards. The Shadow would have had some fabulous put-down that would have shut my dad up, but there you are. You

41

can always think of a stunning retort once you've left the scene. I'll have to write them down. Practise being The Shadow.

I'm going to make a concentrated effort to get some more photographs. Adrian's brother, Ross, has told me about the Dark Web. I've heard of it, but don't know how to get on it. He says he'll show me if I want. It might be the place to show the pictures. I'd already thought about it. Now might be the time, although you don't know who's out there and what they'll do to you.

I thought I might be able to get some pictures here to use, but I've learnt all about this thing called ethics since I've been working as a porter. I have to be ethical in everything I do. I can't talk about people and their problems to anyone, not even my mum. I have to be careful how I speak to patients, even when they're a pain in the backside. Remembering ethics is bloody hard work.

So, because of ethics I have to be creative when taking pictures. Of course, I knew I couldn't bring my camera in and stand about like Ridley Scott, but I do have a brand new phone in my jacket pocket. I can take pictures with it, and with the increase in pay I felt I could afford one. It's not the dearest so I hope it will be good enough. That Ross is a nosy bugger, though. He's always snooping about. I'll have to watch him.

V

'Anyone home?'

'Come in, Pat. You know I am,' Janet called. 'I've put the kettle on. Tea won't be long.'

It was a long-standing arrangement between the cousins that the minute Pat saw Jim leave the house she would pop across the road for a cup of tea and a cake. The women were lucky in that he was a person of habit, leaving for the pub at roughly the same time every day.

'He's later than usual,' Pat commented as she sat herself at the kitchen table. She set a box wrapped in flowery paper in front of her, waiting for Janet to comment. 'Where's he off today, all dolled up to the nines?'

'The Waggon and Horses.' Janet informed her cousin as she poured boiling water onto the tea bags and dropped the cosy over the teapot.

'I thought he was barred from the Waggon after that incident at Aunty Glad's funeral?'

'He was – is – but an old work mate called this afternoon. He said, if Jim sat in the beer garden he'd fetch him a pint. I think it's Pauline's day off. If it is, they might get away with it.' Janet placed the teapot on the table and turned to pick up a couple of mugs.

'And if it isn't?'

'Get ready with an excuse for being here.'

'Right. You'd better have this, then.' Pat pushed the package across the table.

'What's that?'

'Open it and see. I'll pour the tea. Is the milk in the fridge?'

Janet nodded absentmindedly as she turned the prettily wrapped box round and round.

'Come on Janet. It won't open itself.'

'What's it for?'

'I thought you needed a pick-me-up.' Pat hesitated.

She wasn't usually stuck for words, but it was tricky. 'You know. With it being May and all.'

Janet did know. 'Ah, May. It's funny, isn't it?'

Pat waited.

'Mum dying in May. It's like she wanted to keep things tidy. I can push May into a cupboard in my brain and all the really bad things that have happened to me will be hidden away until next year.'

'Oh Janet.'

'You know it's Dad's anniversary today, don't you?'

'I do. 20 years. Where's that gone? Hence the pick-you-up. Open it will you, before his lordship comes back.' Pat picked up her mug of tea and blew the steam from the top.

Janet tore at the sellotape around the edges of the parcel and slid a pink box out of the wrapping. It contained a variety of her favourite toiletries.

'I'd have got you something really special, but he'd only have thought you'd got another man,' Pat sighed. 'Do you like it?'

'Of course I do. I'll just put it in my drawer. The tea will be cool enough to drink when I come down.' Janet quickly bundled the paper into the bottom of the waste bin and dived upstairs to put the toiletries out of sight.

* * *

'Why did you stay with him? I mean – after your dad died.'

'I promised Dad I'd make the best of it. He would never have wanted me to divorce.'

'You mean you wouldn't have considered divorce. Come on, Janet. We're in the 21st century now. How can

44

you still think you'll go to hell for getting out of a disastrous marriage?' Pat was very much a lapsed Catholic. She was against any religion that was misogynistic, forcing women to toe the male line.

'It was the last promise I made to my dad. Anyway, things weren't so bad in the beginning. It's the drink. Jim wasn't drinking so much then.'

'He may not have been as belligerent as he is now, but he's always wandered. Now, he has and you know it.'

'He's genuinely sorry about that affair, you know. And he was devastated about Dad. They got on quite well by the time Craig was born. Both enjoyed the football.'

Pat snorted into her mug.

'Things were okay for a while,' Janet insisted.

'Would Craig agree?'

Janet didn't answer.

'He didn't like another man in the family did he, your Jim?' Pat pushed.

'Things were fine while Craig was little.'

'Too busy wandering, like I said.'

Janet knew that Pat was right. There were two reasons Jim gave any thought to his wife. One was purely for procreation so he could boast what a man he was, and the other was if he couldn't get sex anywhere else. He was barely home while she was pregnant with Craig. She only saw her mother when Jim was out and rarely saw her in-laws. Len was too embarrassed to look her in the face whenever they met. Rene was more sympathetic and helped when she could. In fact, she was the only visitor Jim tolerated and was a blessing when Craig was born.

'Craig's enjoying his new job,' Janet informed her cousin, in the hope of changing the subject.

"I'm pleased for him. I bet they're busy up that hospital.'

'Non-stop, he says. I don't see him so much these days.'

'How are things since your mum – you know …'

'Fine. There's only the two of us now so …'

She didn't need to finish the sentence. Jim had Janet all to himself and all she had to do was follow his routine and all was well. For Jim. Janet had no real life of her own. He didn't hit her, but it didn't mean she wasn't punished if she did something Jim didn't approve of. If he came back while Pat was still there, it would result in questions and no telly for her that night.

She knew Pat would start on again about her leaving Jim, but even if she agreed she couldn't see how she was going to be able to manage it. Pat had offered her a room as her children had all left home and she had the space, but unfortunately she lived across the road from Janet's own home so there'd be no escape. Just more hassle.

Craig lived in a one bed-roomed flat so there was no way she could stay with him.

She had worked in the same job ever since Craig started school, but it was only for a few hours a week in the betting shop next to the Working Men's Club. It was okay at first. Jim was working and she enjoyed the repartee with the other staff and the punters. Unfortunately, Jim wasn't in the habit of keeping a job for long. It wasn't always his fault – she had to give him that – and he always found another. Work did give him structure and he never drank until he'd finished for the day. But firms went bust or down-sized, and as time went on he struggled to find new employment. And once he'd officially retired, he was always around at the bookies, even though he wasn't much of a gambler. Making sure she didn't get any hassle from the punters was his excuse. She was beyond old enough to retire but had carried on as it gave her some time of her own. She only packed it in when her mum became so ill it was obvious she wouldn't recover.

Her mother's neat little bungalow had been sold to pay the fees at the nursing home, and there was barely enough left to cover the funeral costs. She'd managed to hide a bit of jewellery that had belonged to her mother as well as her father's good watch. She'd passed them on to Craig. She'd not got a daughter and, you never knew, her son might settle down one day. She'd ignored the disappointment in his eyes when he saw the meagre inheritance. She had tried to save, but Jim always seemed to find where she'd hidden what little she'd managed to keep. It had all disappeared down his throat.

So she had no money and no one she could turn to. She'd have to do what Pat suggested. Put her faith in God and a runaway number 45 bus.

'Another cup, Pat?'

Work, Work, Work

I don't think this job is such a good idea. Okay, it's more money, but I shall never get the photograph I want while at work. I only ever see live patients and not one who's at death's door. I have to wheel them from A to B. I've elected to work in A&E. Anything can happen there. People die at the drop of a hat. But it's my job to take people from the cubicle they're in to X-ray or a ward.

In the beginning I offered to take a couple of night shifts for a youth with children. Parent's Night or something at their school. Now it seems that people think I'm happy to do all the night shifts. Well, that's an exaggeration, but I do seem to do more than my fair share. This means that I can't get out at night to take photographs.

I've considered offering to work in the morgue, but that won't help as the patients will already be dead. I need to see people at the moment of death for this experiment to work.

I've confided a little with Ross. I haven't told him the exact reason – just said dead people don't bother me if anyone's squeamish. Sort of hinting but he told me porters rarely, if ever, see people as they pass. They're either alive or dead. The doctors and nurses deal with the bit in between. He gave me such a funny look I decided not to mention it again. He probably thinks I'm a necrophiliac.

Then he caught me with my camera in my pocket and wheedled out of me that I was an aspiring journalist looking for the right picture to rocket me to stardom. I suspect he'll use that against me when he needs to. He's a smarmy little git, not like his brother.

So, I'm stuck with nosy old women who want to know all my secrets and men who can only talk about football. I'm not a fan of sport.

I've not attempted the Dark Web. I've googled it but taking that final step seems a bit too much. Not much of an investigative journalist, you might be thinking? The thing is, I will, it's just that I don't need it yet.

I've got some time-off owing me because I've worked bank holidays so that youth with children could spend time with them. He must be a masochist. Anyway, it's done me a favour. I can get out at night again. I'm going to wander about as the pubs and clubs shut. Mingle with the crowd, blend with the shadows. Whatever works.

VI

Craig was on a break, enjoying a cigarette in the smoking booth outside of the accident unit at the hospital when his friend sidled up to join him.

'Want a couple of these?' Ross opened his jacket pocket so Craig could see what was inside.

'Joints?'

'Spliffs. You know that lad who was knocked down by that little old lady?' Craig nodded. 'I found them under the blanket after the police came to interview him.'

'But …'

'He won't dare come looking for them, now will he? Not with the police here.'

'Spose.' And he thought hospitals were safe havens.

'Go on take a couple,' Ross urged.

Craig was tempted. More than tempted because he was planning to get out at night during his leave. He reached into Ross's pocket and took a spliff.

'Take another. Two each then.'

Then I can't dob you in, thought Craig to himself.

'Craig. Craig is that you?' Craig thrust his hand into his own pocket, hiding the evidence before turning.

'Aunty Pat? What's up? Are you alright?'

'Ay'up Craig.' She nodded to Ross who signalled he was going as he wandered back to the hospital entrance. 'I'm glad I've caught you. It's not me. It's your mum. She's had a bit of an accident.'

'When? Why didn't you phone me?'

'I did, but it went straight to answer.'

'Fuck. I switch it off when I'm at work. Forgot to check it. How do you mean – accident?'

'I mean accident. She was rushing back from mine and tripped over the kerb. Banged her head. I thought it safer to bring her here.'

'Did she lose consciousness?'

'Well, possibly. She insists she didn't, but I'm not taking any chances. You know what'll happen. Your dad will expect his tea at the usual time.'

'Tell me about it. You did the right thing, Aunty Pat. I suppose she was worried he'd find her missing.'

'She was whittling about her mother actually. Missing her.'

'If you say so. Did you use an ambulance?'

'No, I drove her. Your Uncle Steve helped get her in the car. Thought it would be quicker. They took her through pretty quickly. Bang on the head at her age, I suppose. I'll wait with her if you're working.'

'I'll come with you. They'll let me stay with her. They're good like that.'

Craig ground out his cigarette and popped it into a little tin he carried for fag ends needing disposal. 'Show me where she is.'

* * *

'Eh, Mum. What are we going to do with you?' Craig asked. He hadn't realised how old his mother was looking. Perhaps it was the fall. She had a nasty looking gash over her left eye where her glasses had sunk into the skin as she hit the ground. She was going to have a right

50

shiner. It was already forming. A nasty purple swelling on the ashen grey wrinkles.

'Broke m'glasses,' she sighed. The speech was slow and ponderous as if Janet was having a struggle to pronounce each word.

'Don't worry about them. We'll sort it once we've sorted you.' Craig reassured her.

'Have y'seen our Pat?'

'She was just here with me, Mum.' Craig was concerned. His mum had just seen her sister in his presence. 'She's gone to get a cup of tea.'

The swish of the curtain caused Craig to turn around.

'Hi Craig, did someone call you? Only I don't think …' the harassed looking nurse asked.

'She's me mum,' the porter informed her. 'Has she been seen by a doctor, only I think she has concussion? She's a bit confused.'

The nurse quickly checked the notes from triage and then took the patient's pulse. 'That eye looks odd. I'll get someone. You stay here. If anything changes, press the button.'

'Now you're scaring me,' Craig half-joked.

The nurse indicated he move away from the bed, as if his mother couldn't hear them a couple of metres away.

'It's possible she had a TIA. I know it says she banged her head, but she might have done that if she fell due to the stroke. Her right eye seems out of line. What's her speech like?'

'She's confused and she has to put a lot of effort into talking.'

'Right. Oh, here's the doctor now. Let's give her room to work.'

* * *

'So she's had a stroke.' Pat had joined Craig for a cigarette in the booth outside of the hospital. 'I'm not surprised. She's always whittling on about something or another. Well, Jim'll have to fend for himself now.'

'Yer think?'

'He will. Your mum will be in hospital.' Pat inhaled deeply.

'She'll only be in a couple of days,' Craig informed her as he flicked ash into his little tin.

'A couple of days? She's had a stroke.'

'It's a TIA and they'll still kick her out with a care plan as soon as it can be arranged.'

'Tell them what he's like Craig. Tell them she'll get no help. That she'll have to carry on looking after your father.'

'They'll need the bed. Pat, I've seen little old ladies – confused old ladies - sent home at all hours of the day and night because they need the bed. She can come to me. I'll sleep on the sofa.'

'No, she won't. She'll come to me. I've turned our Kyle's room into a lovely guest room. She can have that. It's right next to the bathroom.'

'If dad knows she's there, he'll be round.'

'Steve will sort him out. You'll need your sleep if you're working. We've retired now. No problem.'

'Thanks Aunty Pat.'

'What time do you finish? Come for your tea.'

'I should have finished half an hour ago. I'm on earlies this week. I'm going to stay with Mum, though. I'll pick up some fish and chips later. But thanks for the offer.'

'Steve's coming later with your dad – if you're

interested,' Pat told him. He'd not once mentioned his father and how he might be coping.

'I'm not.'

Behind the Indian

I'd look after my old mum because she's stood between me and Dad all these years. Saved me from Dad's strap on more than one occasion. What I never got straight in my head was the fact that he would thrash me for doing the same type of things he had done. Perhaps it was the way I did it.

I'm glad Mum's going to Aunty Pat's. Does that make me selfish? Possibly, but she'll be better off there as there'll be someone in all day to look after her. I'll still need to work. Anything could happen while I'm out of the house. Mum's so independent. Pat says she's not her old self, by any means, but I know she'll insist on getting me a meal for when I finish my shift, and there's one thing I have had drummed into me since I got this porter's job: the home is the most dangerous place on this Earth. You might think that climbing a pylon to mend electricity cables is dangerous. Nothing like slipping on a wet floor with a kettle full of boiling water.

I actually like my job. I never thought I'd enjoy work but I do now. I know I see some dreadful things but I feel needed. Dad never really wanted me. He doesn't like me. I make the effort to go to the pub with my colleagues so I can be one of the gang. I'm not much of a drinker, I've seen what it can do, so I make a beer last all night. No one cares. They've seen what drink can do as well. A& E on a Saturday night is not a place anyone in their right mind wants to be.

Tonight I'm going out for the first time since Mum was taken ill. The hospital's brilliant for giving me the heads-up on areas where there might be trouble. The gossip tells me that there's quite a little camp – if you can call it that – of homeless round the back of the Indian takeaway in Crimea Terrace. Some of the old houses are empty ready for demolition and are perfect squats. Plus the owners of the Indian give away any leftovers at the end of the day. Something to do with their religion and charity.

There's plenty of drinking and drugs going on down there and we've had a couple of minor stabbings in A&E come in from there. With a bit of luck and a fair wind, I might be lucky enough to come across a squabble or an overdose.

Don't judge me. These things will happen whether I'm there or not, and I'm not going to put myself in danger trying to break up a drunken brawl. Especially when there's knives involved. This time, once I've got my photo I'll call it in. Say I was on my way to the takeaway and came across the victim or something.

It's summer and the streets are heaving despite the late hour. I've had to leave it until after midnight due to the light nights. Fortunately, no one's taking any notice of me as I make my way to the back of the takeaway.

VII

''Ere? What's your game?'

Craig nearly ruined his trousers. He hadn't realised there was anyone behind him. It wasn't a police voice. This voice sounded like it was up to no good. When he turned around, he saw that it belonged to an itinerant who looked like he'd stepped out of the set of some dystopian horror film. This youth's dreads reached his backside and, even with only the street lights, Craig could see lice rummaging around inside the hairs. The stranger had made some effort to plait his beard, which was hanging with small bone-shaped beads making him look like a Viking pillager. And, God, did he stink? Craig was so grateful that he'd taken those spliffs Ross had found. Who'd have thought the hospital would be such a useful place to work? He thanked the Lord for the gift. Properly, in like a prayer.

Craig decided that a spliff would not only keep the peace but cover some of the smell emanating from the man. He made to put his hand into his pocket, but before he could even penetrate the lip he found a knife being waved in front of his face.

Strangely his first thought wasn't 'Fuck I'm going to die,' but 'Is this a dagger I see before me?' He put it down to shock and not wanting to believe what he was seeing. Besides the youth didn't appear to be quite with it and the knife was wobbling all over the place.

'Fancy a smoke?' Craig asked. His voice was high, and he was tempted to cough and lower it, but he knew how that would look. He had to show no fear to this person or he'd be fleeced for sure.

'What y'got?

'Only spliffs, sorry.'

'Nothing stronger? Smack? Flake?'

'No.' What could he say to keep himself out of danger? 'I've not seen my dealer tonight.' Why did he say that? He didn't mean it.

'Are yu lookin' f' Mo?'

Craig nodded, although he had no idea who or what Mo was. Considering the context he did presume he might be a drug dealer and no he wasn't looking for him but he wasn't going to admit to that.

'He ain't 'ere.'

That was good as far as Craig was concerned, but instead of saying he'd come back another time he said, 'Will he be long?'

He could have said he'd go into the squat and wait in the hope of finding a quiet, dark corner where he could hide until this youth had forgotten about him. Not only was he not carrying any more money than he could afford to lose, due to the fact it might at any time be stolen from him, he didn't want any drugs of any kind. Surely there were other people about. Someone must come along soon and defuse the situation.

'Gis a spliff and I'll get him.'

Not the result Craig wanted, but as coherent speech had deserted him he fished out a crumpled spliff, straightened it and passed it over.

The youth examined his prize. 'What yu after?'

Craig hesitated. He wasn't sure what to say. Did this youth mean what drugs did he want or things in general?

'What y'want Mo for? Candy? Tar? Poppers?'

Craig's mouth opened and closed like a fish in a bowl.

'If yu let me know, I can tell Mo to bring what you're after.'

It was at work in A&E that he heard the street names of the drugs people had taken, but at this precise moment his mind was now a blank.

Craig had thought he was the Big Man wandering around the back streets of town after dark, chatting to homeless old men and sharing cigarettes and a bottle of voddie. The elusive Shadow who was on top of everything. However, it hadn't taken him long once he started work at the hospital to realise he knew nothing. Life on the streets was beyond anything he'd envisaged and he'd seen some sights. Young girls and youths brought in suffering from hypothermia, half-starved and covered in sores and looking for a bed for the night. Cases of gangrene, sexually transmitted diseases and malnutrition all ended up in the A&E department. People had died.

If it wasn't for his mother, Craig himself might well have been one of those street people. He and his dad were forever at loggerheads, and there had been times when he felt he would be better off in some doorway. It was even worse when he returned home after finishing university. He couldn't get a job in journalism, which made him the butt of his father's snide comments. At least he would be free to be himself and not have to tread on eggshells all the time.

His mother understood how things were and loaned him enough to put a deposit down on a decrepit flat, as well as putting in a good word at the supermarket where she shopped, thus providing him with a job. Okay, the flat was pokey and the job had been boring, but both were a blessing at the time.

Fortunately, Craig was spared any more thought over the drugs as the pair were interrupted by a youth barging into them as he ran around the corner. He slowed momentarily, patted Craig as if apologising, made a noise like a pig and disappeared seemingly through a split in the universe. Craig turned back to his assailant only to find he too had vanished, leaving him alone as a couple of police hurtled around the corner, slithering to a halt in front of him.

Fuck

Fuck! Fuck! Fuck!

I've got a spliff in my pocket.

What would The Shadow do?

He'd be all in black so all he'd need to do is take one step back into the shadows and no one would know he was there.

The trouble is – I'm not all in black and there's another policeman behind me.

Fuck.

VIII

'Good evening, sir. Do you mind leaving your hands where I can see them?'

Craig raised his hands like some bandit in a western movie.

'And you are …?'

'Craig Fanshaw.' Craig was shaking. His arms were already beginning to ache, but he was afraid of putting them down. 'But I wasn't doing anything wrong.'

'If that's the case, we'll soon be sorted and everyone can get off home to his bed. What are you doing here?'

'I'm a journalist. I was looking for a story.'

'Journalist, eh? Not heard that one before. Who do you work for?'

'No one – that is, I'm freelance. Looking for a lucky break.'

'Do you have anything about your person that can confirm this?' The policeman looked like he was trying not to laugh.

Craig shook his head.

'Are you carrying anything you need to tell us about?' the other officer asked.

'I've got a spliff. Just the one.' Craig was thankful he'd handed over the other one. Having just one would be classed as personal use. He might get away with a caution. He'd watched the police programmes on the telly.

'Do you mind showing us what you have in your pockets, sir?'

Craig did mind, actually, but was too frightened to refuse. Not that it mattered he hadn't anything else. Only a few fags and a half bottle of vodka.

He dug his hands into his pockets and froze.

'Everything alright, sir?'

No, everything was not alright. There was something in his pocket that hadn't been there before that little scrote had run into him.

'Sir?'

Craig looked helplessly at the policemen.

'I … I … I don't …' He held out his hands. There was the crumpled spliff and three little packets of a white powder.

He handed them over. 'They're not mine. The little bags – they're not mine. They were planted…'

'Not your night, is it sir?' the first officer told him.

'Craig Fanshawe, I'm arresting you for possession of Class A drugs in a large enough quantity to supply. You do not have to say anything. But it may harm your defence if you do not mention when questioned something which you later rely on in court. Anything you do say may be given in evidence.'

The officer held out the handcuffs and, once they were in place, helped Craig into the back of the police car.

'Do I need a lawyer?' Craig asked.

The two policemen looked at each other as if to say, what have we got here? 'There'll be a duty solicitor unless you have someone in mind.'

Craig had never had cause to consult a lawyer – solicitor, whatever. He sank back into the seat of the police car.

* * *

The police station seemed harshly lit after the dim lights of the street. Craig felt sick and desperate to empty his bladder. How the fuck was he going to prove a negative?

'Please? I really need to use the bathroom,' Craig insisted. 'I'll answer all your questions after that.' The arresting officer, who had introduced himself as PC Croft, nodded.

'Just empty your pockets first.'

He was both surprised and thankful that his good camera was still in his inside pocket. He had expected that it would have been lifted at the same time the drugs were planted. He was also thankful he had replaced the memory card. It was totally blank – no incriminating evidence. Surely they'd realise he was telling the truth about being a freelance photographer and let him go with a caution.

The questions began.

Craig dutifully supplied them with his full name, date of birth, and the address and postcode of his flat.

'Have you had any dealings with the police before?'

'No. Will this take long? I'm on shift in the morning.'

'Working?'

Craig nodded.

'Where?'

'At the hospital. I'm a porter.'

'I thought you were a journalist?' Croft pointed out.

'I'm freelance. I have to eat between jobs.' Craig told him.

'The problem we have is you have enough drugs in your pocket to indicate you might be dealing. That's a serious offence.'

'But they're not mine. That kid who bumped into me must have planted them.'

'Kid?' the duty sergeant looked at Croft.

'There was a kid. Looked like Kit-Kat Kenny. We were chasing him when we found this chappie,' Croft informed him.

'See. And there was another man. Long dreads, plaited beard. Stunk to high heaven,' Craig insisted.

'Sounds like Skunk,' the duty sergeant offered. 'You'll usually find them pair together.'

'How do you know Skunk?' Croft asked.

'I don't. I didn't know he was there. I was trying to get away from him when that kid ran round the corner and bumped into me.'

'There's nothing coming up about a Craig James Albert Fanshaw at the address he gave us,' the duty sergeant reported. Addressing Craig he added, 'How long have you lived there, mate?'

'Eight years and, er a bit.' The duty sergeant looked at him. Craig desperately tried to count the months without using his fingers. He was aware of the officers watching him. 'Nine months,' he half-guessed.

'And where were you before that?'

'Uni. Manchester Met.'

'Okay. Studying what?'

'Journalism.' Craig smothered a sigh. 'I lived in digs in Manchester.'

'What drugs did you do while you were there?'

'Bit a weed. Nothing serious. Money was tight.'

Craig's father refused to help him out while he was studying, as he considered that university was a waste of time. Jim had rarely been in school and never been in education beyond sixteen and, as far as he was concerned, it hadn't harmed his chances. Craig's mother helped out when she could, but she had little money of her own. Craig had to rely on his grant and the money he earned from part-time jobs. It didn't leave much time for partying.

University was a wonder to Craig. He was free of his father and doing a course he was really interested in. Unfortunately as time went on, he had all his enthusiasm knocked out of him by the daily grind required to keep his head above water financially, as well as by the constant griping from Jim.

Now as he finally seemed to be making something of his life, this had to happen. His Mum didn't need the hassle at the moment, but worse than that he hoped to God his father didn't have to find out. He'd never hear the end of it.

Chasing Shadows

The Shadow has no fear of the police.

The Shadow would have styled it out, not got his gob tied up in knots and said things he didn't want to. Then again, The Shadow wouldn't have got caught in the first place. He would have slithered back into the darkness and slid away down the ginnel before that Skunk even saw him. He would never have encountered the police.

The Shadow would only be there for the photographs. He has wits I don't even know exist.

He doesn't do street drugs. He has a dealer who sends a boy around to his apartment with the most up-to-date designer product for him to try.

He'll snort his cocaine with a £50 note while the boy waits. If he likes it, he'll pay up and give the boy the £50 for a tip.

If it isn't to his taste, the boy will have to return it and bring better quality dope.

The dealer will know not to mess with The Shadow.

As it was, I did get caught. The longer I sit in the cell, the more time I have to stew about the unfairness of it all. I am The Shadow. I think like The Shadow. I make plans about how I will get even with Kit-Kat Kenny and Skunk. How I will lure them with the sort of drugs they would never have the wherewithal to buy. The stuff will be so strong that they will never need anything anymore.

I will sit in the shadows and watch as they choke, mouth foaming, bodies convulsing until they finally breathe their last. At that moment I will capture their souls and keep them forever in Purgatory.

Only then will I be able to rest.

I know the police are laughing at me. Thinking I'm making myself out to be something I'm not. Just let them wait. I just need one break. Once I am The Shadow things will be very different. People will dance to my tune for a change.

IX

Craig felt himself lucky to get off with a caution. It meant he didn't need to worry his mum, although she hadn't been of the real world after her stroke. It triggered dementia according to the doctors. More importantly, his father would never have to find out. He was shattered when he arrived for his shift but styled it out, making out he'd had a good night on the tiles, despite it being a school night.

The relief soon evaporated, though, and he smarted at the thought of the time he spent in custody, the need to ask to use the toilet like a child. The sniggers from the officers when he told them he was a journalist. He hadn't planned on going out again so soon but the arrest had made him angry. More angry than he had been in a long long time. It was time he behaved like The Shadow. He would get his own back on Kit-Kat Kenny and Skunk. If he couldn't get the type of photograph he wanted by accident, he would engineer one.

'Ross? You haven't any more er stuff, have you?' he asked his colleague quietly as they were waiting to take a patient to a ward.

'Stuff, our youth?' Ross said aloud. 'What do you mean by stuff?'

Craig turned his back to the cubicle and hissed into Ross's ear. 'Shh. Someone will hear you. You know full well what I mean. Have you?'

'Not on me but I can get something. What do you want?'

Craig hadn't given it proper thought. He'd just been stewing but Kit-Kat was a name given to ketamine. Surely that would do.

'Some ketamine?'

'See you in The Dragon after work.'

Craig nodded.

* * *

Ross was sitting in a corner, tucked away from the other punters when Craig entered The Green Dragon. He looked around as he waited for his beer, and it took a while for him to pick his friend out. He'd forgotten to ask how much the drugs would cost. He hoped he'd brought enough. He had every penny he owned in his pocket. Still, his Auntie Pat would feed him and his poor old mum would insist on giving him some pocket money as if he were still a child.

'Did you manage to get sorted?' Craig asked as he pulled up a chair in front of Ross.

'Aye, lad. If you're still up for it.'

'I forgot to ask how much the job would cost.'

'What are you whittering on about? Job?'

Craig looked around him. The pub was virtually deserted. There really wasn't any need to be surreptitious.

'Have you got what I asked for?'

'Indeedy.'

'How much?'

'A couple of hundred mils.' He opened his hand and quickly closed it but not before Craig had seen two small phials. 'Liquid okay.'

'Spose.' Craig didn't know much about drugs. The ones Kenny had put in his pocket had been powder. He was aware that ketamine came in different forms. It was used in the hospital for pain relief and as an anaesthetic, and he suddenly became suspicious as to where Ross had got this from.

'Where did you get it?'

'The least you know the better. It'll be 50 quid if you still want it.'

'Fifty?' For a moment he wondered where Skunk or Kenny would get that sort of money but then realised that it would be through stealing or dealing. He pulled the notes out of his pocket.

'Hang slack, lad. I'm off for a slash.' Ross nodded towards the conveniences as he got up. Craig realised that he was expected to follow. He hesitated as he reached the door. What did he really know about Ross? Was he going to rob him?

'Get in, lad. There's no camera in here.' Ross held out the phials in his right hand and held out his left for the money. 'There, that was painless, wasn't it?' he quipped as he folded the cash and pushed it into his back pocket. 'I'll buy you a drink if you're stopping.'

Craig didn't really want another drink, but felt that it was only polite not to rush off. That would have looked suspicious. He daren't ask for a half, so forced a second pint down.

Ross was chattering away but Craig wasn't listening. He had got on well enough with his brother Adrian when he worked in the supermarket, but they never met socially. He was grateful to Ross for helping him get his job, but now the youth seemed to think Craig owed him.

He disappeared when there was any shitty job to be done, and when he *was* about he treated him like he knew nothing. He was beginning to get on Craig's tits. He had left home because his father was always pulling him down, bitching at him, sniping and ridiculing. He had left the supermarket because Snape was doing the same. Now Ross thought he was fair game.

Craig tended to run away from conflict. His father had beaten any backbone out of him as a child, but just lately ... well, just lately he was beginning to feel the anger welling up inside.

'Well? Well?'

'Eh? What?'

'I asked where you usually get your gear?'

Craig didn't really do drugs. He liked a smoke when he could afford it. He'd even been thinking of growing his own. A couple of plants on the window sill. His mum used to visit occasionally, but she wouldn't know what she was looking at. He spent all his money on his hobby.

'I er don't have a regular supplier.' That, at least, was the truth.

'I could help you out there.'

Craig didn't really want to continue the conversation. He was itching to get out and find the pair that had stitched him up. Ross might join them if he carried on.

A Lightbulb Moment

I didn't manage to get out last night and it was perhaps just as well. I was seething by the time I left that wanker Ross, but it wasn't all in vain. I did get the drugs, although they were a bit more expensive than I thought, and I did have a stunning idea.

I am going to become The Shadow. Now. Instead of waiting for a breakthrough. I'm sick of being taken for granted, shat on by anyone who thinks they're better than me. Well, they've pushed too many buttons this time.

I'll show them.

I really want a black latex gimp suit. That would put the fear of God into them. It'll cost, though, and I haven't the money at the moment, but I know how to do it cheaply for now. It means waiting for the real thing, but I can use that time for planning.

I have some black trousers and shoes. Mum bought them for me for Gran's funeral. I have a black hoody somewhere as well. It will have to do for now. I just need a black balaclava and gloves. Mum loves knitting. Auntie Pat says she still knits. She'd knit all the time if she could, although it's always baby clothes. I don't know why. We have no babies in the family at the moment. I'll ask her to make me a black balaclava instead. I can cut up an old shirt to make a mask in the meantime.

I'm going to try it out tomorrow.

X

'Well, if it isn't David Bailey?' a dark blue voice announced behind Craig.

He was working the night shift, and it was about that time the drunk and disorderly were taking centre stage in A&E. A number were accompanied by police, a usual sight.

Craig turned, and came face to face with PC Croft. He wanted to ask what the policeman was doing there, but the words failed to materialise. It was a silly question anyway. The fact that he was handcuffed to a blood-covered individual who looked as if he didn't know if he was on this earth or fuller's meant that he was escorting some reprobate who had been injured.

'How's the day job?' Croft sniggered.

'This is the day job,' Craig snapped. He was still smarting over the arrest, and now it looked like others would know about it too. Ross, in particular, would want to know how he knew the policeman.

'Sorry, mate. I couldn't resist,' Croft apologised. 'Good of you to try and make a go of something you enjoy doing.' He sounded genuine, but Craig was saved from answering as the gentleman attached to PC Croft was called to have his wounds attended to.

Ross sauntered up as he predicted and indicated the policeman. 'He a friend of yourn?' he asked.

''No, not really.'

'Only I thought you might have a couple of plod in your back pocket.'

'Why should I do that?'

'For when you're out dealing.'

'I don't deal.'

'Whatever. Are you still spying on folk? Snapping them when they're not looking? So you can get the sort of pics ordinary people might not have access to, if you know what I mean.'

'No, I don't know what you mean. I just like to photograph life as it happens. Nothing shady – if you know what *I* mean,' Craig snapped back.

'Sorry I'm sure. Just being friendly.'

'Hey Ross, you busy?' the staff nurse called.

'Sorry, just on my break.' Ross waved at the nurse as he turned and winked at Craig. He sauntered off leaving Craig to take the patient to the bed allotted to him.

Craig's shift went from bad to worse. He preferred the day shift because it gave him the time to go out after dark and look for scenes to photograph. He hadn't gone out since his brush with the police, and it wasn't for the want of trying. It would have been nice to have the chance. He was getting more and more anxious about catching up with Skunk and Kit-Kat Kenny. The fact that they set him up was preying on his mind. The evenings seemed to be full of people who didn't really need to go to an emergency clinic. He could not understand why folk felt it was okay to use the NHS as a social club. He had little patience with the time-wasters in A&E, and it seemed that he had more than his fair share of them tonight. Ross was noticeable by his absence, but at least the time passed more quickly while he was busy.

Craig was just thinking he deserved a break; it was well past time when he was called to cubicle five. PC Croft and his detainee's cubicle. He was to take them to the X-ray department. That meant a walk in the company of the policeman who had arrested him. The last thing he wanted was for someone to find out what had happened the other night. He enjoyed this job; he got a lot out of it. Information on places to visit when looking for photo opportunities for instance. And so far he had not blotted his copybook. It wasn't him who'd taken the spliffs from a patient. He wanted it to stay that way.

'So what's with this photography malarky?' Croft

asked as they walked the long corridor to the X-ray department.

'Jobs in journalism are hard to get,' Craig told him. 'For every one advertised you get a hundred applicants and then some.'

'Cutthroat business, journalism,' Croft commented.

'It is.' Craig was well aware he wasn't pushy enough to be a really famous journalist, but he was good at photography. 'I really want to be a photographer. I keep hoping I'm there when something momentous happens. That I can capture it. Be recognised for it. You know.'

'I'd say find something less harmful than fraternising with drug dealers. It's dangerous hanging around crack dens,' Croft warned him.

'I wouldn't have thought Craig Fanshaw had the guts to go hanging around crack dens,' the chap sitting waiting for an X-ray commented.

'Bob.' Craig was flummoxed. What the hell? This was the last person he wanted to see. Bob Colclough was a friend of his father's from way back and just as nasty. 'What are you doing here?'

'What do y'think? Waiting to have me bloody hair curled.' Bob rubbed his bald head. 'How's your dad? I've not seen him for a few days. I'll have to pop by. I'll be off work with this wrist.'

The policeman hadn't actually said anything about what had really happened, but in a way that was worse. Craig was well aware that what wasn't known as fact was made up in gossip. Bob had a mouth like a blue whale and no respect for the truth. By the time Jim Fanshaw got the tale he would probably be a notorious crack dealer wanted by Interpol.

Craig hadn't been to his family home for a while, not since his mother had had her stroke, and he wasn't planning to go anytime soon, but he did need to see his mum. Some days she didn't know who he was, but on others she fretted, and he didn't want anything to upset her. She knew she had a son called Craig. The problem lay in the fact that she was with her sister, who lived directly across the road to his father. His visits weren't regular due to his shifts, but Jim Fanshaw had nothing to do but watch the goings on in the street. Craig knew as sure as the New Year follows Christmas that his father would be waiting for him.

He felt in need of a treat. His clothing was ready. He would go out tonight after his shift, even though it would be very late.

Nothing. Nada. Zilch.

There is no sign of Skunk or Kit-Kat Kenny.

I venture back to Crimea Terrace and the squat, but there is no one about. Either outside or in. The police must have cleared it the other night and I've not heard where they've moved to.

I'm tempted to get a takeaway and see if the staff had any idea, but I'd used most of my money buying the ketamine. And I'm dressed all in black with a hoody and mitts. I look like I'm on my way to a break-in.

I glide around in the shadows for a while. Practising being The Shadow. Slinking unnoticed past a group of old men around a small fire. They are eating chips, and the smell makes my belly rumble.

Would The Shadow's belly rumble? He would be able to

control it. Then again, he wouldn't be hungry.

I stop and turn and watch from the dark side of the alley for a while, but the men seem to be getting on well. No sign of conflict. They have beer but not enough to get drunk, just amiable. I wonder whether to join them but decide against it. They're nothing to me and I need this picture, but it doesn't feel right, spoiling their night.

I wander across town to another hotspot I have heard about, but those there are all asleep. I can't really see their faces, but I know I would smell Skunk if he was there.

I have my knife. I could easily do away with one of them without the others knowing. I've not killed a human before – just vermin…

.. and animals I didn't like. Noisy bastard dogs barking through the night …

…and breathe.

I don't really want The Shadow to be a murderer. I want him to be above that sort of thing, a help to the community. A person others look up to. Clean and wholesome. How would it look if the person who donated money for a refuge had done something as foul as killing anything? This isn't MarvelWorld. It's difficult to keep such behaviour a secret in real life.

Dad always found out.

Besides it's so messy.

XI

The cupboard was bare. No bread, well there was but it was the shade of green bread shouldn't be, and the milk came out in lumps. Craig managed a cup of black coffee, but that tasted funny and when he looked at the use by date he realised why. There was only one thing for it. He looked at the clock. It wasn't too early to call on family. He had work later and should really have tried to get some sleep, but he was too hungry for that. He'd go to his Auntie Pat's and see his mum. It would be better going in the morning because if his father had been on the beer the night before he'd still be in bed sleeping it off.

* * *

'You're an early bird, our Craig. Your mum's hardly finished her breakfast.'

'I'm working nights all this week. Thought I'd drop by before I go to bed, Aunty Pat. See how Mum is. How you're coping.'

'That's good of you, lad. Want a cup of tea?'

'Yes please. Is that toast going spare?' Craig was positively salivating at the sight of the discarded piece of toast.

'Eh lad. Where do you put it all? Go on I'll do you a breakfast. I suppose you haven't had time yet this morning.' Pat rummaged in the breadbin. 'You go on in. She's in the front room.'

Janet was sitting in her recliner, her breakfast half eaten on a free-standing tray in front of her. She didn't look up as Craig entered the room.

'Ay'up Mum. Ow at?'

Janet continued to stare at the television, even though it was switched off. Craig walked in front of her. 'Mum?'

'Is that you, Jim? Do you want your tea? I won't be a minute. I'll get it for you.'

74

'No Mum. It's me – Craig.'

'Craig? What you doing home from school?'

Craig was well aware of his mother's dementia but had not seen her this bad on previous visits. He desperately wanted to shake her and put her right, but knew it wouldn't do any good. The medics said it was better to go along with her when she was really bad. Even so, he was glad when his Auntie Pat bustled in with a tray loaded with a mug of tea and a plate of poached eggs on toast, which she perched on the coffee table. He wasn't sure he could have restrained himself. Instead he said, 'I was hoping you'd knit me a balaclava, Mum. In black.'

'So you think you're grown up enough for a big boy's balaclava do you?' She stared at him just as she used to when he was a little boy and had done something to 'disappoint' her.

Pat squeezed his arm. 'Sorry,' she mouthed. Craig shook his head. His mother was getting worse. 'Just agree with her. I'll get her to knit you a bally if you need one,' she whispered.

Craig took a deep breath. 'Yes, Mum. I need it for school.'

'I'll get you some wool shall I, our Janet? It'll give you something to do.'

'Well, I did say I'd make a nice little cardigan for our Pat's latest. Do you think she'd mind waiting?'

'No dear. I'll let her know when I next see her.'

Craig turned and left the room. Pat followed, sensing he wanted to talk.

'She wasn't this bad the other day. I know – I know she has good days and bad days, but this is another level. What's happened?'

Pat turned to the sink in a pretence of washing up the breakfast things. 'Nothing different,' she told him.

'Look me in the eye and tell me that,' Craig demanded. 'He's been over, hasn't he?'

'Well yes, but he didn't do anything. Just wanted to see if she was any better.'

'And when he saw she wasn't?'

'Well, he did get a bit put out.'

'He went totally ballistic,' Steve said as he came in cradling a bottle of milk. 'Sorry but I overheard as I came in. We nearly had to call the police, we did. Tell him how it is, Pat. Nothing will change if we keep making excuses for him.' He pushed past Craig and put the milk in the fridge. 'Upset your mum and your Auntie Pat. I'd have lamped him one, but it would have only made matters worse.'

'He'd had a drink, Steve. He's not so bad when he's sober.'

'This can't go on.' Craig made for the door.

'Don't do anything daft, lad,' Steve warned him. 'You know what he's like. He'll make out it were all your fault and he's as likely to get the police involved as not.'

'And you've not eaten your breakfast,' Pat reminded him. 'Go and get it down you.'

Craig hesitated, but it wasn't the thought of breakfast, even though he was very hungry. It was the mention of the police that made him think. Bob Colclough wouldn't have had time to go and see Jim, but he could have phoned him. He was positively gloating by the time he was called for his X-ray last night. Craig wasn't sure he was ready to face the self-satisfied reaction his father would have when he was told that his useless son had finally become the failure he always thought he would be. Even though it wasn't true. Craig was not one for conflict, but buttons had been pressed. He would be able to retaliate without his mum being on the receiving end of the consequences.

Craig was shaking with rage and ready for revenge.

But this revenge was going to be served cold. And he was going to enjoy it.

Revenge

A movement out of the corner of an eye. It is hardly fully dark. The street lights make sure of that. But the street lights cast shadows where things of the night lurk and shift. Silent as the bats that wheel and dive, the movement nears the middle house in the street. The night is warm with no breath of air.

It is darker at the back of the house with no chance of being seen this close to the walls. Light pressure on the door handle. The drunken sod had forgotten to lock it. No need for the key. Nothing has been moved. No danger of tripping over rearranged furniture.

There is light deep inside. Just the television left on, the sound turned low. Some bizarre celebrity show. The shadows watch for a while. The occupant is asleep. His mobile phone in his lap. Interesting.

The phone disappears into the blackness. Still the man sleeps.

Where is the fun in that?

The dark shifts, morphing into human shape. It stands in front of the television and picks up the remote control from the cluttered coffee table. Turns up the volume.

Sound reverberates through the house.

'Hey! I'm watching that.'

No response.

Through the alcoholic fog, the man suddenly realises that there's a strange person in his house.

'Who the fuck are you?'

No response.

'Get out of my house.'

No response.

'I'm calling the police.'

The shape waves the mobile phone in front of him.

'Is that you, our Craig? Daft sod.'

The figure in the chair tries to get up, but he's had a few beers and is quite drunk.

The Shadow stretches out an arm, the mobile phone held tantalisingly close. He uses it to push the old man back into the chair.

'Think you're bloody clever, don't you? I know it's you. Dressing up like Batman like you're still some snotty little kid.'

No response.

'High on drugs, are you? Bob told me all about it. Hanging round crack dens. I always knew you were a bad 'un.'

No response.

'Go on. Deny it. T'wasn't me, Dad. Don't beat me, Dad. I won't do it again, Dad.'

No response.

'We all knew it was you. Well – except your mother. Butter wouldn't melt as far as she was concerned.'

No response.

'No one could keep a pet round here. Not 'til you left.'

The darkness steps closer. The old man sinks back into his chair. 'Go on then,' he cajoles. 'You haven't got it in you. Always was a wimp when it came to real people. You can't rely on your mother anymore. Your shenanigans have sent her do-lally.'

He realises that the black shape before him is dragging something from the waistband of his trousers. It snags as he pulls. Throwing the phone across the room, he tries again.

'Huh, you can't even do that properly,' the old man sneers as he watches the hammer materialise in the glow of the television.

'Fitting last words from you,' The Shadow growls. 'That's all I ever heard all my life. Just watch me.'

Once he starts, The Shadow couldn't stop.

XII

Craig was aware someone else had entered the room, but he was too tired to move, sitting in the chair his mother used to use, opposite the bloody carcass that had been his father. Both hands clutching his phone. Whoever it was turned off the television.

'Eh, lad. What have you done?' Receiving no answer the person squatted down in front of Craig. 'Can you tell me what really happened? The police should be here soon. We need to get this straight.'

Craig stared at his Uncle Steve as if he didn't know him. A single tear slid silently down his cheek and landed with another dark stain among the blood splatters on his T-shirt.

Steve's phone began to ring. An old-fashioned bell. He

tapped it to answer. 'No, don't come over. Craig and his dad have had a set-to.' Pause. 'Look I need my attention here for a bit.' Pause 'There's no sign of the police yet.' Pause. 'Yes, yes, I will ring them again. You worry about Janet. I'm going to wait here. I'll explain when I can.' Pause. 'I can't leave them, Pat. I just can't' With that he hung up on his wife and turned to Craig.

'Are you ready to talk, our Craig? I'd make a cup of tea, but I don't think I should touch anything. I've already turned the telly off.'

* * *

Steve realised that some time had passed since he'd originally phoned the police. That call had been about the noise. Perhaps they didn't take noise as seriously as he had hoped. Perhaps they were very busy. He tapped in 999.

'Emergency, which service do you require?'

'Police, please.' While waiting for the police to answer, he did wonder if he should have called for an ambulance as well, but a police caller interrupted his thoughts.

Steve hardly heard the caller's voice. He just blurted out, 'There's been a murder. He's dead.'

The police caller patiently talked Steve through what he knew, and he had only just finished answering the questions when there was a loud rapping on the front door.

'Open up. Police.

* * *

The officer quickly evaluated the situation and put in a call. The central light went on and Steve could see the full extent of Jim's injuries. He thought he was going to throw up and quickly turned away.

'My name's Croft. PC Croft. Who are you and how are you involved?' Steve turned towards the voice and shook his head.

'I heard the noise. He's my brother-in-law. I came across to tell him to turn the noise down.'

'Who let you in?'

'I let myself in. The backdoor was open. Not just unlocked but open. I turned the telly off. Is that alright? I know I shouldn't touch anything, but it was getting on my ti – nerves.'

'Don't worry about that. The deceased … do you know him, then?' The policeman looked across at Craig. 'Do you know the youth?'

'It's my nephew, Craig Fanshaw.' He eye-pointed at Jim without really looking at him. 'His son.'

'Is there anyone else in the house? Wife?'

'His wife has had a stroke. She's with us – across the road – convalescing.'

He became aware of more people filling the house but was finding it difficult to process anything.

'Are you alright?' Another officer touched Steve's elbow. A young woman who looked as if she should be with her family doing her homework.

'No, I feel sick. A bit wobbly.'

'I'm taking him in the kitchen. Putting the kettle on. It's not part of the crime scene, is it?'

'Well, they did enter through the kitchen door. I'd say take them down to the station. Give the pathologist room to work.' Croft's gaze took in both Steve and Craig.

'I can't get anything out of Craig,' Steve told the

police. He knew he was whining but couldn't help himself. 'He won't talk.'

'It'll be shock. We'll get the medics to check him over before we question him. Are you okay with that? It'll be better than here, I promise you.'

'I had nothing to do with it.' Steve was suddenly worried that he might be accused of helping Craig.

'No one is accusing you of anything. We just need the facts.'

'I need to call my wife. Tell her where I'll be. She's already worried about the noise.'

'Can it wait?'

'Not really. She'll be over if I don't. I don't want her to see this.'

'Okay. Just tell her you're helping the police. No gruesome details.'

Steve's hands were shaking so much he had trouble finding Pat's number. She picked up immediately.

'I'm with the police. I might be some time.' He didn't wait for an answer but shut his phone down. He hadn't the headspace for anything else.

A sudden yell followed by a scuffle caused everyone to turn.

Craig was gripping his phone tightly to his chest. Eyes wide with terror, lips curled in a snarl.

'I only asked for the phone,' the young officer explained. 'He refused,' she added lamely.

Croft swung round to Steve. 'Is he involved with any political movement?'

Steve nearly laughed but stopped himself. 'No, not our Craig. He was hankering to be a journalist. A media photographer – whatever.' Then it dawned on him. 'He wouldn't know how to blow somebody up. He's not that savvy.'

'There may be useful evidence on that phone, though. We need to remove it.'

'Here, let me,' Steve urged.

'It's not really the done thing.'

'It'll be alright. He knows me.'

Croft handed him some latex gloves.

'Sir?' The young officer was wary of allowing a member of the public to put himself in danger.

'It's okay. I had dealings with this youth a couple of weeks ago. I doubt there'll be any danger.' He turned to Steve. 'Don't push it. If it looks like he's getting too upset, stand back.'

Steve nodded and pulled on the gloves like he'd seen on the television.

'Eh, our Craig. We're in a bit of a mess here. Do you want me to look after that phone for you? Put it safe like?'

Craig stared at Steve as if he had no idea who he was.

'I got it,' he told his uncle. His face relaxed and it reminded Steve of the little boy he used to take to the park once upon a long time ago. His smile broadened across his blood-splattered face. He held up the phone like a trophy. 'I got it.'

The Shadow

I am The Shadow and I do as I please. No policeman is going to make me do anything I don't want to do.

I got another picture. I haven't had a chance to look at it yet because the police spoilt everything. They have the phone with the pictures of the old man's death. I need that.

I don't know where I am. It's too bright and smells of piss, disinfectant and school dinners. There's always someone in my space. They keep asking about the phone. I tell them to look closely at the last picture and they'll see what I mean. They keep asking me, over and over and over. They're too stupid to see it. I ask them to let me look at the picture and I can show them what I mean, but they don't. They keep saying they want me to tell them.

They say all they can see is a dead body, battered and bloody. But it is there.

I'm going to need that photograph for my exhibition. They ask about the exhibition, but I won't tell them. The exhibition will speak for itself, I tell them. Come and see it for yourselves. Come and see what I see in the photographs.

They ask about Craig's father and his mum. I tell them I'm The Shadow, what has it to do with me? Then they try to make out that I'm Craig Fanshaw. They say Craig killed his father. So what, I tell them. He was a bully. Got what he deserved.

I want to see my mum. Uncle Steve came to visit. He says she's too poorly, but I want to talk to her.

Don't worry, Craig. I'll look after your mum for you. Once they see what I've achieved there'll be plenty of money. I'll get the best doctors for your mum. Soon everyone will see what was captured in that second death struck. The soul, spirit, call it what you will, leaving the useless body.

Human essence looking for a new host.

Evie's Friend

I suppose it all started with the doll and went downhill from there. Our little girl was not a child who played with dolls, even though her grandmother had bought her one as a gift. Nor did we push gender-specific toys, but after the birth of her little brother the doll appeared from its hiding place under her bed.

Despite our best-efforts Evie, our three-year-old, was convinced that her new sibling would spring fully grown – well the same age as her, at least – and female from her mummy's tummy. We did our very best to make her feel included and special, but she was decidedly put out when Elliot put in his noisy appearance, especially as he was too tiny to play with her.

'Is Dolly joining us for lunch?' I asked Evie. It was a few days after the birth, and she was arranging her doll's plastic limbs with such enthusiasm that I made a reminder to self to make sure she could never be alone with the baby. She crushed the toy into the dolly's highchair she had pushed next to her.

'AlliDrider,' she emphasised, 'wans duop.' I understood this. It meant that the toy, named after our next-door neighbour and my good friend Alison Driver, wanted some soup, and I turned to fetch another bowl. I was happy to play along to keep the peace. The sleepless nights were already racking up and Evie no longer slept during the day. I was exhausted and was down to tackling each minute as it came. I expected this doll-as-family-member would end as suddenly as it had started once she began Pre-school in the fast-approaching September.

A pattern was set with AlliDrider substituting for the longed-for sister and going everywhere we did, Evie pushing her little doll's buggy alongside me with her brother in his.

She mimicked my actions so constantly, bathing, changing, and expecting a portion of our meals for the doll that I was surprised one morning, only a few days later, to see it was missing.

'Doesn't AlliDrider want her breakfast?' I asked as I poured cereal into Evie's special bowl. Evie stared at me as if I wasn't making sense.

'Doll's don' teat *food*,' I was told in no uncertain terms. 'Ginnie wan's cornflakes.' Evie nodded towards the empty chair beside her. 'Wi' sugar.'

So, Evie had given up on the doll and now had an imaginary friend. I smiled to myself as I poured a few flakes into another bowl, splashed on some milk and a few grains of the sugar I kept for visitors. I believe I had an imaginary friend when I was little too. Mother didn't like it much and I soon learned to keep quiet about it. I decided to be more magnanimous. As I was putting the packets away Elliot woke, so I left Evie to her breakfast and went to fetch him from his crib. I was only gone a couple of minutes, the baby being in the next room, but by the time I got back both bowls were empty.

'Gosh, someone was hungry,' I said.

'Ginnie says you din put nuff sugar on.' Evie told me.

'There's sugar in the cereal. You don't need more,' I

said firmly. Evie banged the table loudly making Elliot jump.

'Ginnie wans more sugar!' she shouted as the baby began to cry. It was looking like it was going to be one of those days.

The next day didn't start too well either. Evie looked rather pale and sat listlessly at the table, although she did insist on a bowl of cereal for Ginnie.

'Are you feeling poorly?' I asked, but she just shook her head. 'Eat your breakfast, there's a dear. We can go to the park as soon as Elliot's ready.' I was busy with the baby, and when I turned back to Evie, I saw that, while her bowl was still full, Ginnie's was empty. So that was the game, was it? At least she'd had something to eat. I leant over the table to pick up Evie's bowl and could have sworn I felt a small hand touch my arm as it passed the chair next to hers. I decided it was just tiredness. Wasn't sleep deprivation used as a torture?

The day continued quietly. Evie remained pale, but she ate at lunchtime – albeit everything on Ginnie's plate rather than her own when my back was turned filling the dishwasher. As my gaze swung from Evie to the empty plate and back again, I was sure I saw something out of the corner of my eye. A shadow standing by the empty chair, but it was gone when I looked specifically.

'Baby brain,' I chided myself and thought no more of it.

Over the next twenty-four hours Evie became a worry to me. She was very pale, her skin translucent with dark patches beneath her eyes. I considered taking her to see the doctor, but she played happily with her new imaginary friend giving me time for the household jobs while her brother slept. I could hear her chatting away nineteen to the dozen as she built some strange construction using Duplo. She was eating, sleeping and there was no temperature. I decided to give it another day or two. Appointments were so difficult to get, besides which it was the start of the weekend, and it was hardly an emergency.

I started putting more food on Ginnie's plate and less on Evie's; that way I could ensure she had enough to eat if she was going to carry on with that game. I could have insisted she ate from her own, but why create hassle when there's no need? I had a new baby, and Gareth, my partner, was working all hours so I could be a stay-at-home mum. You can't have everything. I told myself it was a phase, and it would pass. Allie Driver told me so, and she'd got three seemingly well-adjusted children, so she should know.

'Who's that with Evie?' Gareth asked on Sunday morning as he yawned his way over to the kettle, hair like a toilet brush, pyjama bottoms sagging unbecomingly.

'No one. Unless she's talking to her imaginary friend,' I told him. Ginnie was becoming quite the inconvenience, her virtual presence getting stronger.

'I'm sure I heard someone in the dining room with her. They're under the table playing house.' Gareth didn't seem particularly concerned, but my partner didn't often see the finer points of child rearing. To his credit, he probably presumed it was Alison's youngest, who sometimes came to play. I heaved myself to my feet and went to have a look. He was right about one thing. There clearly were voices, more than one by the sound of it, coming from under the table. As I moved further into the room, I felt a cold draught brush against by body as if someone had hurried by too close for comfort. A shadow rolled across the room, like a cloud across the sun on a summer's day. I felt a fear – of what I didn't know, but I dropped quickly to my knees in order to look under the table, sure that Evie was in trouble.

'Hello Mummy. Ginnie's gone to the shop. Do you want to play?' It struck me that her language was developing rather rapidly. I had a cup of tea going cold in the kitchen, but felt such an irrational fear that I wanted to stay and see what happened when Ginnie came back from the shop. She didn't; at least she hadn't when Elliot woke demanding a feed. I reluctantly left Evie to it, but didn't shut the door so I could hear what was going on from the kitchen.

All remained quiet. I could hear the mumble of voices from the dining room, the chatter from the front room as Gareth Skyped his parents in New Zealand, and the hum of the fridge in the kitchen as I sat nursing Elliot while I stared at, without seeing, the cold cup of tea. All seemed normal, but somehow I felt that it wasn't.

Monday morning was always a rush to get back into routine after the luxury of lazing on Sunday. The usual, 'Why didn't you put it ready last night?' and 'If you knew you needed it, why didn't you look for it before this?' meant that I didn't really look closely at Evie until Gareth had left for work with the hustle and bustle following him like rats from Hamblin. I sank in my chair. Elliot was cooing happily in his crib, so I turned my attention to my daughter, my hand on the jug handle ready to pour her some milk. As my gaze swung from baby to Evie, I was convinced that I saw someone sitting in the chair next to her. I was so convinced that I gasped, and the milk splashed onto the plastic tablecloth. But Evie was alone. It was her appearance that frightened me now; she looked very poorly. I could see her veins through the paleness of her skin. Her eyes looked huge and there were dark circles beneath. I didn't hesitate this time but picked up my phone and rang our surgery.

We managed to get an appointment quite quickly with Evie being such a young child. The doctor thought she might be anaemic, despite not finding any other symptoms other than her lack of colour. He said he would arrange for her to see a paediatrician at the local hospital if things didn't get any better and was I getting enough help with the new baby? Enough rest? A proper diet? I don't know why he questioned me so closely. Having two little ones was bound to take its toll. I answered curtly and left. We managed to fit in a blood test for Evie using the promise of the park as a reward. I was on pins waiting for the results, which came in the next day. All clear. I didn't believe them for one minute, but Gareth persuaded me that I was an anxious mum and to give it some time. If things didn't improve, then I could make another appointment. He certainly wasn't as concerned as me.

Evie continued to eat from Ginnie's plate, but I felt that she was losing weight. Her little bones showed through her translucent skin, and on Friday morning her knickers fell around her ankles as she played in the garden. As I went to help her, I felt a presence slip between us. It was forceful enough to stop me in my tracks. A child. It was a child, I was convinced of it. I felt as if I passed through it, and the feeling was cold and shocking.

Evie was upset by the goings-on in the garden and refused the milk and biscuits I put out at snack time. It wasn't long before both children fell asleep, Elliot in his crib and Evie on the front room settee. As I sat at the kitchen table with a large cup of tea to steady my nerves, I found I was staring at the chair next to where Evie usually sat as if willing myself to see someone sitting there. Someone malevolent.

I started suddenly as if woken from sleep. I felt sure I hadn't been asleep and that I had not taken my eyes from the direction of the plate, but the biscuits I had put out earlier had gone. I looked up at the chair and saw a dark shape forming. A giggle rolled around the kitchen. A hand touched my shoulder, and I nearly passed out with the shock.

'Sarah? Is everything alright? Only, I could hear Elliot as I walked by.' It was Allie, my next-door neighbour. She was looking rather anxious, more so when I started to cry. 'Goodness, you look dreadful. What's up?'

I could hear Elliot yelling at the top of his lungs, and Evie was standing in the doorway with a defiant look on her face sucking her thumb, so I indicated I needed to deal with them.

'I'll put the kettle on.' Allie pushed her three and Evie through the open back door to play in the garden and proceeded to take control.

I couldn't tell my friend about the shadow child; she

would think I was mad. I let her think it was concern for Evie, but I knew what I saw. I felt better after a cup of tea and a chat about the perils of bringing up children, and Allie decided she was satisfied enough to leave me to get back to my routine.

At teatime I filled Ginnie's and Evie's plates with chicken nuggets, chips and beans; and then, instead of clearing up while they ate, I sat and watched. I watched as the shadow formed, more distinct now, definitely a child. I watched the food disappear into the shape. I could see features now, dark hair in bunches, a button nose, a red jumper. Enough. I jumped up, startling Evie and causing the ghost child to vanish like the Cheshire Cat. Only her giggle remained.

I decided that this ghost child was trying to take my child's place, and I was not going to let her. But I didn't know what to do. Would anyone believe me? She had disappeared when Allie came in, but Gareth had heard her. Would he see her?

The conversation with Gareth was difficult. More difficult than I thought it would be, considering he had heard two voices in the living room at the weekend. Obviously, he thought I was suffering from postpartum depression, and had decided Evie had been putting the other voice on. We agreed I should see the doctor. Well, Gareth insisted, and I agreed because I was tired and it would keep the peace. We also agreed that, as it was the weekend, Gareth would take charge and see what happened. Perhaps I did just need a rest, but that wouldn't explain Evie. I promised I'd reconsider the doctor on Monday.

It was sheer bliss to lie back on Saturday morning as Gareth struggled out of bed. I stretched and listened with a smile on my face as Evie explained to her father exactly how he was to change a protesting Elliot's nappy.

'Daddy, Mummy doesn't do it like that.' I missed Gareth's reply.

'Put one hand on Lelliot's tummy and then you can do it.'

I couldn't help but smile. Evie was developing into a proper little madam.

All too soon, he came back into the bedroom and deposited a red-faced, dry but not exactly wholesome baby in the bed.

'You'll have to feed him,' he said apologetically. 'I don't have the necessary …' He circled his chest with his forefinger, before disappearing downstairs to see what Evie wanted.

I don't know if I dozed off or not, but it didn't seem a minute before the crash of breaking crockery startled me and Gareth appeared white-faced and shaking.

'You've got to come down. Now!'

Elliot was asleep but still latched to my breast and it didn't do his temper any good to be woken, but my partner looked terrified.

'What's the matter? Is it Evie? Is she alright? Has she cut herself?' I threw the questions at him as I passed the baby to him, swung my legs out of bed and found my dressing gown. He didn't answer but kept telling me to hurry and I'd see.

He let me go first. Evie was sitting at the bottom of the stairs looking paler than ever and petrified, but she grabbed my hand and walked just behind me, clutching tightly. The kitchen was a mess with broken bowls, cereal, sugar and milk everywhere.

So much for my day of rest! was my next thought as I insisted they all get out of my way and leave me to set about cleaning the kitchen. I didn't want anyone to cut themselves and add blood and the possibility of a hospital visit to the mayhem. But the thought I really needed to consider I pushed to the back of my mind, unable or unwilling to deal with it.

By the time I had finished the kitchen, all three were asleep on the settee, so I showered and dressed before making a fresh pot of tea, adding biscuits, and sitting down in the easy chair opposite my family. Gareth was awake by then – just.

'Well?' I said as I poured. 'What happened?'

He struggled to a more comfortable position without disturbing Evie. He was taking his time, thinking how to put it. When he saw I was still waiting, he sighed and began. 'Everything was fine. I did it all how you said. More cereal for Ginnie – then a voice said, "I want more sugar than that."' He looked at me expectantly, but I didn't say anything, so he carried on. 'I thought it was Evie at first, you know, putting on a voice, but the language was so clear and more adult than Evie's. Anyway, I told her she had had enough, and all hell broke loose. The bowl went flying, the box of cereal tipped over and the sugar bowl and milk jug – well you know. God, Sarah, what's happening?' I didn't know but I was scared, very, very scared.

It seemed that this Ginnie was getting stronger as Evie weakened, so I persuaded Gareth that we needed some time out. I felt that we needed to get away from the house and the situation, and suggested we to go to my mother's for a while. I felt we needed somewhere neutral in order to talk and plan. This showed how desperate we were as my mother had never liked Gareth, continually remarking about how he would never commit to marriage, despite it being our joint choice not to, and actively criticising how we brought up Evie. She hadn't even been to see Elliot, citing the fact that she lived too far away. Nevertheless, we packed quickly, booked into a B&B, so as not to put her on the spot, and left before lunch.

We ended up leaving within a couple of days as Ginnie had come with us and continued to be her demanding self the whole time. My mother refused to believe that it wasn't Evie being naughty, citing spoilt-child syndrome and continually reprimanding her, which ended up in a family argument to top all family arguments. I think the B&B owners breathed a sigh of relief as well, although I had given way to Ginnie's demands to keep the peace. They gave us some odd looks when I asked for a place setting for her. Through it all, Evie got – dare I say it – more and more transparent.

Once we got back, I suggested looking into the history of the house, just in case there had been some sort of horror incident in the past. Perhaps the house was haunted by some poor child who had been unlawfully killed.

'Come on, Sarah. What planet are you on?' Gareth scoffed. 'Have you thought your mother might have a point? You know as well as I do that Evie's struggling to accept her new brother. Her behaviour's hardly perfect.'

Now there was some space between him and Saturday's incident, he had decided that there was a rational explanation.

'What do you know about it? You're at work all day.'

'Perhaps I am, but we need the money.'

'I know that, but I have Elliot all day and at night as well. I get up so as not to disturb you. I'm bloody tired. You could do your bit at the weekend.'

'I play with Evie so you can get on,' he sulked.

'That's big of you,' I snapped. I wasn't enamoured of my free time being used up with household tasks. I needed a break. Our argument woke Elliot and he started to cry. I stormed out of the kitchen to go and see what was bothering him, slamming the door as I did so.

Later when we had both calmed down, I again raised the idea of researching the house. This time Gareth's reaction was one of cynical amusement, but he nevertheless agreed. I suppose he thought the research would keep me distracted until we found out the real cause of Evie's illness.

Alison was a good help as she had lived in the street for a number of years, but nothing untoward came to light through her. The houses had been built in the 1930s, making them ninety years old. The elderly lady we had bought the house from had been married for nearly 60 years and she and her late husband had lived there for all that time. They raised two sons, who were successful in their respective fields, and she had gone to live with her eldest granddaughter when she felt she could no longer cope on her own. She couldn't remember the family they had bought it off, but no doubt they had died by now. She knew of no accidents, suicides, or untimely deaths of small girls. Nor were the houses built on an old cemetery or plague pit.

All this while Ginnie was getting stronger. I saw her more often, and not just out of the corner of my eye. She would be sitting watching me as I mused while feeding Elliot. As often as not, I would speak to her instead of Evie. My child would look hurt, but I didn't care. It reached the point that I didn't even care that I didn't care.

I found some clothes among my shopping one afternoon that I had no memory of buying. I panicked for a moment, wondering if I had been shoplifting without realising it. What would be the consequences of that should I have been caught? I had bought a red dress, a pair of shoes of the same colour and some pretty white socks with frills. I had the receipt, but why would I have done that? They were far too big for Evie. I hid them away, scared I was losing it.

I found I had no time for my little daughter. I was too busy looking out for Ginnie until … 'Mummy?' I turned and stared. 'I don't like fishes. Fishes make me sick.' Evie made a retching noise.

'Of course you do!' I snapped. 'Eat it. Eat it all.' I was watching the chair next to her. I could see the child sitting there with a grin on her face. She ate all her fish, cleared her plate like a good little girl.

The smell of vomit brought me back to earth. Evie sat with tears streaming down her cheeks and a lapful of regurgitated fish.

I cleaned her up quickly and gave her a cheese sandwich, which she sat and looked at, hiccupping quiet sobs. I stared at her as if I didn't know her.

That night I dreamt. I dreamt of Ginnie's birth as if I

had been there. As if I had given birth to this little monster, who wasn't a monster in my dream but a perfect little baby. Perfectly formed and beautiful. I woke sobbing with Gareth shaking me, worried for me.

'What the hell, Sarah? Is it a dream? Nightmare?'

'I know who she is,' I stammered. 'Ginnie. I know who she is.' Gareth looked puzzled. 'She's Poppy.' I burst into tears.

'Don't be silly,' Gareth paled noticeably. 'Poppy? No way.' But he clung to me, and we wept together until we fell asleep.

We both woke feeling hungover, but the children were awake and needed feeding. 'We need to talk about this,' Gareth said looking at the teapot on the breakfast table.

'Stay home today,' I pleaded. 'Help me.' I was beginning to fear that I was causing all this because of Poppy. He nodded and fished for his phone in his dressing gown pocket.

'I feel like crap anyway,' he muttered as he keyed in a number.

Gareth phoned in sick, and we got all the routine tasks out of the way. I sat Elliot in his rocker and Evie in front of CBeebies with her favourite book while Gareth made more tea and then we sat, one each side of the kitchen table as if afraid of each other. We were about to relive Poppy and that was going to be hard, so hard.

I had been pregnant before Evie. Gareth and I were ecstatic, as were his parents when we told them the news. My mother expected that we would marry as there was a baby on the way, but neither of us believed in marriage for the sake of it and this caused quite a rift. We didn't speak again until Poppy.

I was thirty-two weeks into the pregnancy and, apart from the family issue, there had been no problems. It was a bank holiday and we had been to tea with friends. Afternoon tea at Paul and Nigel's included lashings of cocktails, various ones all based on gin. Being pregnant I stuck to orange juice, and therefore was obliged to drive the two of us home. I was standing by the driver's door waiting for Gareth to roll down the garden path when a speeding car swung around the corner on the wrong side of the road. It tried to swerve but clipped our car and knocked me over.

I delivered our baby later that night. We called her Poppy and, arms wrapped around each other, held her as she died.

I was ill and scared for a long time after that. I needed physiotherapy for the physical injuries, and we both had counselling for the loss of Poppy. The court case awarded us a reasonable compensation, which helped with the additional expenses incurred. My mother blamed me for my unchristian relationship with Gareth and Gareth because *he* had had a drink when visiting *his* friends, ignoring the fact that I'd introduced them. She never once offered sympathy or help and refused to come to the funeral as the child had been born out of wedlock.

Now Poppy was back, after six years, to join the family she had lost.

I had told the counsellor that I was coping at the time, because all I wanted to do was shut it all away. I did cope, or at least pretended to cope, because I didn't want my mother to crow about the effect it had on me and my relationship with Gareth. We went through a bad patch, but got over it with help from friends, and I believe we are stronger for it. We pushed the past behind us and tucked the mementos of her short life away. We made Evie with our love, and now we had Elliot. A perfect, balanced family – and Poppy wanted to join in.

'I've brought her back,' I wailed to Gareth by way of a start.

'Don't be an idiot. How can you have brought her back?' But I saw him look towards the chair where I could see Poppy was sitting, smiling. He just looked puzzled.

'I can't bear to think of her on her own and unloved.'

'Of course, she's loved,' soothed my partner. 'We will love her until the day we die.'

'But there are times when I don't think of her at all,' I hiccupped. 'She's come back to haunt me.'

'You've got a toddler and a baby to look after on top of a husband,' he tried to joke. 'You won't think of everyone all the time.' He looked back at the chair and then at me. He grabbed for my hand. 'Tell me, Sarah, what do you see? I'm sorry but ...'

I stopped him. Gareth didn't believe in ghosts. He was probably too sceptical to see. 'I see,' I said, staring at Ginnie/Poppy. 'I see a little girl of about six years, dressed in red ...'

'Don't ghosts come back as they were when they died?' Gareth butted in. 'I mean, I don't know about these things, but Poppy was a tiny baby, a few hours old. Would she come back as a six-year-old?'

'I don't know. I've never thought much about ghosts either.' Not before this.

'What else do you see?'

'She has brown hair that glints with red in the sunlight. It's tied in bunches with red ribbons. She has hazel eyes and a button nose. Oh Gareth, she's so like Evie.'

'What does Evie see?' asked the ever-practical Gareth.

'I don't know. I've never asked her,' I admitted.

'Perhaps we should.' Gareth leant back in his chair and called through the door. 'Evie, can you come to Daddy for a minute?'

Evie trotted in. She would never refuse her father. 'I 'aused the telly,' she told him wisely.

'Good girl. Evie, you know your new friend Ginnie? What does she look like?'

Evie stared at him as if he was a penny short of a pound. 'She's a girl.'

'What colour hair has she got?' I asked gently. 'Is it like mine or Daddy's?' I have chestnut hair, tied back in a ponytail, while her father's is black and curly, a testament to Maori blood way back in his family.

'Like Mummy's but tied up in two tails.' Evie indicated both sides of her head.

'What is she wearing?' I asked.

'Jumper like Leliott.' Elliot was wearing a red jumper that day.

'Thanks Evie. You go back to your telly now.' Gareth gave her a kiss on the cheek and a pat on the bottom as she giggled off towards the front room.

I waited until I heard the television. 'Do you believe me now?' I asked.

'I never said I didn't believe you,' Gareth insisted. 'I'm pretty sure I heard a child with Evie that Saturday; I just thought it was Evie putting on a voice. And I don't really know for sure what I saw when I refused to give her more sugar.'

I nodded satisfied I was not hallucinating.

'But it is hard to swallow,' Gareth continued. 'The ghost bit, anyway. I always believed you could see something.'

'Why? Because I had the crazies after Poppy died?'

'Don't talk like that. It was traumatic. It was only through the grace of God I didn't join you.'

'I thought you didn't believe in God?' I shot at him.

'It's amazing who you turn to in times of trouble,' he admitted. 'The real question is – what do we do about it? And we do need to because it seems to be harming Evie…' he continued.

'Are you saying *I'm* harming our daughter?' I was angry, mainly because I felt that he was right.

'No! No, not intentionally but something about this is.'

'Perhaps we should get more tests done on Evie. They may show something.' I don't know what I was trying to prove.

'And what if you put her through that and they show nothing to be wrong?' he asked.

'They will. Because Poppy wouldn't hurt her sister.'

Gareth looked at me thoughtfully. 'Do you want to keep this Poppy?' Said like I'd brought a puppy home. 'Because it seems to me you can't have her and Evie.' He was getting angry, I could tell, but trying to control it. I could see the red spots on his cheeks, a sure sign.

'Do you want to get the exorcist in? Father Ted?' I was getting hysterical.

'Stop it, Sarah. Don't be silly, it doesn't help. I think we should start with the doctor. You should see the doctor – you did say you would. You can talk it all through with him. Then let him decide what to do. I'll make an appointment asap - and I'll come with you.'

'To make sure I go?' We were arguing in hushed whispers, trying not to upset the children.

'No. To support you. I think you need more emotional support than I can give you, and you'll need to start with the GP.' He was very firm now and I was getting tired, so I gave in and left everything to him.

The GP ran through the usual questions: was I eating the right foods? drinking plenty of fluids? getting rest and exercise? did I have help? He then referred me to Mental Health Services without any need of persuasion, all the while talking to me in what I considered to be a condescending manner, and telling me that such things were very common, and they'd soon have me sorted out. Gareth and I pulled faces at each other as he turned to the computer to key in an update on my notes. He also prescribed Prozac, which I knew I wouldn't take even as he told me that the local chemist would have it ready in a couple of hours. At least we were doing something.

Gareth spoilt things at teatime. I left him with Evie while she ate her tea, and I went to change Elliot. A dreadful noise from the kitchen had me running to find him sprawled on the floor beside an upturned chair with a lapful of fish fingers and peas and a nasty gash on the side of his head. Evie was crying in great big gulping sobs.

'What the hell's happened?' I was too scared to care about the children hearing my language. I put Elliot in his rocker, picked up the chair and went to help Gareth to his feet. He pushed me away as I went to make him sit on the chair, and chose one the other side of the table. He was shaking and pale. I picked up my phone.

'Who are you calling? I'm not going to hospital.'

'I'm phoning Allie to have the children. And you are. That's a nasty head wound. Did you black out?' Elliot was crying by now as well as Evie, and I didn't have to say a word to my friend.

'I'll be round,' she said as soon as the connection was made.

Between us, we made sure that Gareth could not refuse to go to A&E. Allie's husband was home, and she elected to stay at our house so that the children had the least disruption possible. I mopped up the wound, which was bleeding well as head wounds do, and gave him a clean tea towel to hold against it.

'They'll ask me how it happened,' Gareth muttered as I drove him to the hospital.

'How did it happen? You weren't showing off to Evie, were you?'

'No.'

'Well?'

'I don't really know for sure, but I sat on the chair next to Evie. The one she usually keeps for this Ginnie. This is the truth, Sarah. I thought I sat on something. Something squishy and warm.' He paused for breath. 'I leapt up and there must have been something on the floor because I slipped, and the chair went one way, and I went the other and banged my head on the corner of the cupboard. I didn't know what to say so said nothing, but my mind was working overtime. 'I can't tell them that, can I?' he said.

One silly excuse, six stitches and five hours later we arrived home. Allie and her eldest, eleven-year-old Lily, were nearly asleep on the settee watching some rubbish on the telly.

'The children are in bed. I think they're asleep. They're quiet anyway. You haven't done too badly for time,' Allie said.

'No, a bleeding head wound got us seen quite quickly,' Gareth quipped.

'What's the verdict?'

'Slight concussion and stitches,' I told her. 'Thanks, Allie. How about you, Lily? It's so late for a school night.'

'You know how Evie loves her. She popped round to help and then fell asleep herself, didn't you, duck?' Allie ruffled her daughter's hair much to her disgust.

'Was Evie alright? Not too upset?' I was very concerned for my daughter.

'Well, she was crying, but she let me get her ready for bed and read her a story,' Lily told me.

'Elliot was okay with the bottle,' Allie said stretching. 'We'd better go see how Dan has coped with the other two. You take care, Gareth. See you tomorrow.'

I let her out, showering her with thanks and then turned to my partner. 'You can go to bed too. I'll just check on the children and then I'll join you.'

Evie was not asleep. She started to cry when she saw me and sat up holding out her arms. I snuggled her closely. 'I don't want Ginnie to be my friend anymore,' she hiccupped. 'She hurt my daddy.' I wasn't sure if it was wise, but I had to ask her if she saw what had happened. 'Daddy was going to sit by me, but he sat on Ginnie, so she moved the chair and he fell off.' I didn't question her but just hugged her tightly. I could have cried as I felt her little bones in my arms. When Gareth had asked me if I wanted to keep this spirit Poppy, I wanted to say yes, but he was right she was dangerous. I was still torn between my need for my baby girl and the need to do something radical before someone I loved was seriously hurt.

I'm not religious. I had too much of it rammed down my throat as a child. My strict upbringing came about through old school religion with 'spare the rod and spoil the child' at the centre. When I met Gareth, I found a way to free myself of much of the guilt and lack of confidence this had given me. We decided that if the children mentioned anything religious, we would answer as truthfully as we knew how and leave them to make up their own minds. We kept Christmas and Evie knew the story of the Nativity, we all loved our Easter eggs, but that was it. We were all a bit pagan, if anything, in the way we celebrated the festivals. If we were considered hypocrites then, tough, but Gareth's remark about turning to God in a crisis made me think, so in the morning I got up early and hunted out the child's prayer book my mother had bought Evie for the christening she never had. I placed it carefully on the seat that Poppy/Ginnie used. If Evie didn't want her as a friend, then we'd start by moving her away. I'd seen the films. If crucifixes and holy water did the trick, then perhaps a prayer book would do the same.

Gareth, followed closely by Evie, thundered downstairs to find me sitting in the middle of what looked like an explosion in a confetti factory. I was too numb to cry, too numb to even feel.

'What the fu…'

'Daddy?'

Gareth cut off his expletive and hunkered down beside me on the floor. 'What happened?'

I shrugged and indicated the mess. I couldn't bring myself to speak. I looked helplessly at my partner. 'Could you… do something? I'll sort the children.'

I ran a bath and got in with the children. It was a tad cool for comfort, but it seemed to soothe us all. When we finally got downstairs Gareth had cleaned the floor and vacuumed up enough of the paper pieces to find the kettle and toaster and make comfort food.

Over tea and toast and marmite I explained what I had tried. 'Perhaps I should leave. Just go away.'

'That will solve nothing,' Gareth retorted. 'We need a solution. Have you heard from Mental Health?'

'Not yet. There'll be a waiting list. Others worse off.' I glared at him. 'But this isn't a mental health issue.'

He didn't give me eye contact. 'Humph, I'll phone, and lay it on thick and say you'll take a cancellation. That this is upsetting everyone and harming Evie.' It was still early, but he kept trying until someone answered, and the result was an appointment in two days' time. I left him to it. It kept him out of my hair. 'It's a good job you're not suicidal,' muttered Gareth as he shut down the phone. I wasn't so sure anymore.

Despite my thoughts on the subject, I went for my appointment. I felt I could do with talking things over with someone who was not emotionally involved. I was a bit apprehensive as I walked into the reception of the Mental Health clinic. I hoped that Gareth's high-handed attitude hadn't upset things. I knew how easy it was to colour an opinion of someone. I was on my own. I felt that I had been abusing my friendship with Allie, and so Gareth stayed home with the children.

Doctor – call me Marie – Chapman was very reassuring. For a start, she had read my notes and was up to date with my history and sounded empathetic rather than pitying, which relaxed me, but I still wasn't sure how to broach what I considered to be the problem.

'You're holding something back,' she announced eventually. 'You must tell me everything – be honest. I can't help you if you don't do all you can to help yourself.'

'It's difficult,' I muttered. 'I don't know how to put it.'

'Just blurt it out,' she advised me. 'I'm not here to judge. We can unpick it over time.'

'I have what I call an ability.' I waited and so did she allowing me to fill the silence in my own words. I took a deep breath. 'I sense things – outcomes – before they happen.'

'You think this is having an adverse effect on your relationship with your family?' I realised then that she would have to know the full story, not only what I'd told my doctor, which was that I was struggling to ensure Evie's safety.

From an early age I had been able to sense things by touching an item, especially if there was a strong emotion attached. Sometimes I would dream of an incident and it would happen. I would use this ability in times of stress and sit and zone out until I visualised the outcome of the stressful situation. It gave me comfort and a feeling of being in control. Gareth knew about this, but rationalised it by saying that I was picking up on clues in the world around me and formulating an outcome. Whatever.

I foolishly told my mother, who then tried to thrash it out of me, telling me it was wicked and against God and that I was an evil child. So I hid it from her – along with a lot of other things.

How do you tell a rational human being this?

'Can I start from the beginning? Put it into context?' She nodded.

'We'll have some coffee. And I think I've got some biscuits in a drawer somewhere.' She called through to reception, and shortly a tray appeared through the door carried by the smiling receptionist.

Once settled, I told Marie all about what I had initially considered to be my daughter's imaginary friend but had turned into a malignancy with a life of its own. I told her about Evie's deteriorating health and the fact that I was concerned that I had formed that evil entity because of my ability. It was as I'd hoped: once I had begun, I found I couldn't stop the flow. I needed to get it all off my chest, to tell it to someone. I had no adult family other than Gareth, and only Allie as a good enough friend to trust with some of the family secrets. Eventually I confessed to my relationship with my mother, and how I had bottled up my grief over Poppy because of her attitude.

'The brain is unexplored territory,' Marie explained. 'We don't know half of what we could be capable of if we discovered how to use more of it.' She at least seemed prepared to believe me.

'Do you believe, through what you call your ability, that you created this, this Poppy?'

'Yes.'

'If you created her, surely you can control her? Unmake her?'

I hesitated. We were back to the question Gareth had posed. Did I really want to get rid of this Poppy? Marie was waiting, but the more I thought about it the worse I felt, and the tears began to fall silently and oh so fast. She pushed a box of tissues towards me.

Eventually I felt in enough control to smile crookedly at Marie, who was waiting quietly. 'Here's the thing,' I said. 'I want Poppy. I want her desperately, but I do know it will hurt Evie …' I stopped because I didn't want to admit that there were times when I didn't care what harm I caused as long as I could have my firstborn back. 'I'm a bloody mess, aren't I?' I admitted.

'You haven't been through the grieving process, and that has upset things,' Marie told me. 'You've come a long way today.'

'What will happen now?' I asked.

'Well, you have choices. We could continue to meet. If we do that, I would like to see you more frequently.'

I nodded thoughtfully.

'There are drugs …'

'No, no drugs.'

'They are just to relax you. I think you are showing severe symptoms of postnatal depression, and you really need to talk this over with your family.'

'What are the other options?'

'I could refer you to a psychiatrist. Your symptoms are severe. Look, I'd rather talk to both you and your partner.'

'Why?'

'I think there might be something more going on than I can help you with. I'll make another appointment. Please bring your partner.'

I wanted it sorted so I had to agree.

'She thinks I'm nuts,' I told Gareth when I walked in. 'She wants to see us both on the next visit. She's scheduled me for Wednesday at two o'clock. Can you make it? I don't think she'll see me on my own.' He just nodded.

We spent the week appeasing Ginnie and encouraging Evie to eat morsels of her favourite foods. We became split as a family. Me feeding Ginnie and Elliot at the kitchen table, and Gareth feeding Evie in the living room. Tempers became frayed, the children picked up on it and became fractious. I even considered the Prozac.

I didn't know what to expect from the next visit. Coffee and biscuits were supplied and the box of tissues handy. Marie cleared her throat and began. She asked that we listened first and then we could ask our questions and we could thrash things out. She explained that she thought I had an associated disorder called postpartum psychosis brought about by a number of factors, the death of Poppy being the main one, and kick-started by the birth of Elliot. She told us that I would need further tests to confirm it but it would explain my delusions and hallucinations.

'And what delusions and hallucinations would these be?' I asked coldly. 'Because Gareth's seen things too and ...' I held up my hand as Marie was about to speak. '...and so has our next-door neighbour.'

'Fathers can have postnatal depression as well,' Marie continued.

111

'What about the neighbour?'

'I can't possibly comment as I wasn't there,' Marie replied. She was obviously out of her depth. She certainly didn't believe us.

'Perhaps you had better refer Sarah to someone who can help,' Gareth suggested quietly.

'No,' I snapped. 'We'll go private. We'll sort this out.' With that I stood and walked off. Gareth shrugged a sorry at Marie and followed me.

'We still have some of the compensation money,' I said as we walked to the car. 'What better reason do we have for spending it.' It was a statement, not a question.

We were at a bit of a loss as to where to start. After the fuss with Marie, we wanted to be sure we were going to be talking to someone who would listen and evaluate our situation without prejudice. We knew no one who had used a privately practising psychiatrist, and had no yard stick. Fortunately, we had a sympathetic doctor who knew my history well and was able to recommend someone.

One major advantage of paying for treatment was that after our initial consultation in his rooms Dr Gray asked to come to our home as he wanted to see the whole situation. We elected for the children's teatime, so he could see for himself what was happening.

I was concerned that he might not show, but right on time I opened the door to the big burly man with a merry face and jovial laugh. He was very good with Evie and soon had her eating out of his hand.

'She's a bonny wee lassie,' he smiled.

'Not so bonny now,' I complained.

'Do you mind if I record as we go along?' Gray had taken out his phone. 'It's less intrusive than note-taking. I'll delete the file as soon as it's written up, I promise.' I shrugged. 'Excellent. Shall we start with the children's tea? I can see someone who's starving.' He grinned at Evie, who immediately clambered into her chair.

Gray insisted I carried on as usual and not just sit and chat. He even helped, for which I was grateful as I wasn't so self-conscious that way. He asked me not to point things out but to let him get a feel for the atmosphere.

Gareth managed to get away from work on time for a change and joined us at the end of tea.

'How did it go?' he asked warily as he walked in through the back door. I was on my own filling the dishwasher.

'Typical,' I snorted. 'Nothing happened.'

'He won't just make a judgement on one visit,' he said. 'Where is he?'

'Watching CBeebies with the children while I clear up. He wants things to be as normal as possible.'

'Are we paying him to watch TV?' snapped Gareth.

'It's only been a few minutes. We're waiting for you.'

Gray must have heard Gareth come in and joined us in the kitchen.

'The baby's asleep and Evie's watching the television,' he told us, 'leaving us free to chat. Good evening, Gareth.' I flicked the switch on the kettle and joined the men at the table exchanging pleasantries while it boiled.

'What do you think of these?' Gray said suddenly, taking us by surprise, as he turned his phone screen for us to see.

'When did you take these?' I asked. They both looked at me. 'When? You can't take pictures of my children without consent.' I was furious.

'I asked if I could record, you acknowledged it.'

'I thought you meant conversation. Anyway, when did you take this picture of Evie? I only gave permission today.'

'Look at the date, Sarah,' Gareth said quietly.

It took me a while to actually focus on the date. Both men sat patiently and watched me in silence until I did.

'You've done a – a thing with it. That can't be today. You've seen her.'

'Sarah, love. It is today.' Gareth stroked the back of my hand. I snatched it away.

'She doesn't look like that. She's … she's pale – transparent! Poppy's taking her over. You've seen it. You've seen what she's capable of.'

I felt rather than saw Dr Gray get up. Gareth moved closer and put his arm around me. I felt myself slipping, I was so tired. I could hear Gareth saying something soothing but couldn't understand the words. Suddenly I rallied.

'What about the clothes? The clothes are too big for her. Her knickers fell down.' I scrambled up and headed for the utility room, where I fished in the laundry basket. I pulled out the clothes Evie had been wearing and took them into the kitchen. Gareth took them from me and spread out the little knickers. He showed me the label.

'Five to six years,' he said quietly. 'She's only three.' His eyes were wet.

'What about Ginnie – er – Poppy? You've seen her. You said you'd seen her,' I wailed.

'I haven't *seen* her. I've seen the mayhem but not a figure,' he admitted.

'Evie's seen her. Told you about her. What she looks like.'

'Evie told me that you told *her* what Poppy looks like.' I didn't like the look on Gareth's face. 'Dr Gray thinks you need a bit of a rest.'

'I do not need rest!' I shouted. 'What I need is someone to sort this out.' I spotted Evie standing by the door, thumb in her mouth, face red and blotchy from crying. 'You're making me upset Evie now.'

I felt pressure on my shoulders and gave in and sat. 'You need a rest, Sarah,' Dr Gray soothed. 'By doing that, you'll be helping Evie.' I said nothing. 'If you resist, I'll have to insist.' He pushed a cup of tea in front of me, and I pushed it away.

'You're not drugging me,' I snapped.

The voice was soft and soothing. 'I wouldn't drug you without your knowledge or consent, Sarah. That wouldn't be ethical, but you do need rest.' I stopped fighting. I was feeling tired all of a sudden. 'We'll arrange a nice rest for you with nothing to worry you,' Gray told me. Had he drugged me, despite what he said? I tried to get up from the chair, but couldn't. I couldn't think. I could hear the men talking, but I didn't understand them. I just needed to sleep because then this would be a dream and when I woke up everything would be fine.

I watched Gareth leave the kitchen. He took Evie with him, and when he returned he had my overnight case and no Evie. I wanted to cry, but hadn't the energy.

When the car came for me, I let them help me into it. Gareth had to stay with Evie and Elliot. He would have his hands full with two small children, so Poppy came with me. It was for the best.

The Boyfriend

All individuals have their own perceptions of reality and that is fine. It's what makes us the diverse people we are. I would no more expect anyone to intrude on my acuities than I would enter theirs. Take murder for instance, some people say it is wrong.

I've heard people talking about me at work. I've listened sometimes when they don't know I'm there, standing quietly in the corner, by the photocopier. They shut up and move away when they see me watching but that's alright, as long as they leave me alone.

I find office mentality banal at best, if not downright embarrassing at worst. I have no wish to make the acquaintance of the fly-by-nights who work in mine.

I have many friends and we converse at our leisure when the work of the day is done. We socialise face-to-face, as opposed to telling all on some so-called social media page that isn't social at all because it does not involve any of the unspoken minutia of discourse. We can express a hundred words with a raised eyebrow, a pursed lip or wry smile.

I may seem obsessive, but that is because everyone else is so lackadaisical. When I look around at the mess people live and work in, I could commit murder.

December

Lisa woke to a banging on her front door followed by the sound of a key in the lock.

'Who was that?' shouted a familiar voice. Her friend Kaz had clumped noisily into the tiny flat, dropping the spare key onto the coffee table. 'Sorry, have I woken you?' she called, but she didn't sound at all sorry. She took Lisa's discarded dress from the settee and dropped it on top of the key. She picked up a shoe, two fingers pinching the strap, and grimaced as she let it fall to the floor.

Lisa carefully inched from her bedroom, head pounding, body wrapped tightly in her duvet. 'Bloody hell, Kaz. Do you have to talk in riddles this time of the morning? What are you doing here anyway? What time is it? What day is it? Is social media down?' she wanted to know.

'You look like someone's just reanimated you. Facebook's fine, so is Twitter, Instagram, and all the rest as far as I know. And it's Saturday, you're alright, no work.' Kaz dropped untidily onto the settee she had just cleared and turned on the television.

Lisa stumbled in front of the screen and turned it off. 'That had better have been some *do*, the way I feel,' she mumbled as she sank into the armchair. 'How come you look so sprightly?'

'You probably can't remember anything. I was designated driver.' Kaz grinned. 'A bore at the time, but it has its upside. It means I can drink in the New Year as I shan't be asked again for a while. You, on the other hand, did have a skinful and are now paying for it.' Lisa would have nodded in agreement, but it hurt too much.

'So, how did it end?' Kaz cast her friend a wicked grin, finally revealing to Lisa as to why she had really called in. 'You and that fella you picked up?'

'Gotta pee.' Lisa jumped up and disappeared down the narrow passage, into the bathroom and locked the door, smiling to herself. He was fit and then some. 'Put the kettle on,' she called, wincing at the sound of her own voice.

Kaz was leaning against the kitchen sink engrossed in her phone when Lisa emerged from the bathroom wrapped in a towelling robe. The girls had known each other since their high school days and were more like sisters than best friends. They both went to the local university, and now found themselves working together in the pathology laboratory in the regional hospital. Pathology might sound highly technical and glamourous, but screening bloods and other unmentionable substances became pretty repetitive after a while. The glamourous stuff was sent elsewhere.

Kaz shut down her phone, and they settled at the breakfast bar which served as a divider between the kitchen and the sitting area. 'So ...' She took a breath. 'Tell your Auntie Katherine everything. What's his name? Age? Where does he live? Why haven't we seen him before?' She passed her friend a mug of strong, steaming tea and a box of paracetamol as they perched on stools at the tiny bar.

'His name's Harry. We didn't discuss ages. He works in the orthopaedic department, not ours. Came with a friend, or so he said.'

Kaz smirked but said nothing. Lisa continued, 'He says

there's never been a reason for him to come into our lab. He's only been with us for a short while; that's probably why we haven't seen him before. He's not a fan of corporate mentality, he did tell me that. He doesn't normally attend works parties as he finds the choice of music banal.'

'Is that why you disappeared?' Kaz asked grinning widely. 'Because he didn't like the music. I've never heard it called that before.'

'You have a one-track mind,' Lisa snapped. 'Anyway, we don't all have sex on the first date.'

Kaz shrugged as if to say it's only a matter of time. 'Are you seeing him again?'

'I hope so,' Lisa enthused.

'What do you mean "hope so"? Didn't you arrange anything? Exchange phone numbers?' Kaz was incredulous. She would definitely brag about knowing everything of interest by the end of the first date.

'He doesn't have a mobile,' Lisa explained.

'Is he for real? No mobile. What about Facebook? Surely, he's on some sort of social media? What about Tumblr?'

'Says not. He doesn't do technology outside of work.'

'Could be just an excuse,' Kaz mused.

'An excuse?' Lisa really wasn't up to this level of interrogation with a hangover.

'Not to get back in touch. You were a lot drunk,' Kaz reminded her friend knowingly.

'Whatever.'

'Is he worth it, you have to ask yourself.' Kaz looked thoughtful.

'Give it a rest, Kaz. *I* picked him up at the staff do,'

Lisa reminded her. 'He might have just been at a loose end. Not wanted to seem rude. If I see him about, I'll apologise for my drunken behaviour and be friendly, with hope we can take it further. When, or if, I get to know him better, I'll tell you if it's worth it.'

Kaz was thoughtful for a moment. 'It's a good job you met him through work.'

'And that's good because …?' Lisa sipped her tea. She was starting to feel more human.

'The missing women.'

'Oh them.'

'What do you mean "oh them"? It's getting scary. Anyone could be next.'

'For goodness sake, Kaz. You've got a very warped interest in these missing women. I bet if you looked at the stats, you'd find nothing out of the ordinary. There's always someone going missing.'

'Except it's more than one,' Kaz reminded her.

'Two,' Lisa reminded *her*. 'And there's no connection between them. One of them was a sex worker, for goodness sake. Hardly the safest profession.'

'So they say – or not say. The police don't tell the papers everything. That way they can sift out the time wasters and attention seekers.' Kaz, who liked to watch police programmes on the television, had formed a morbid fascination with the missing women and kept trying to outthink the police. 'Two women have gone missing in quick succession and they were both from around here. Anyone could be next. That and they can't even get any CCTV footage that could be of any help.'

'So they say – or not say,' goaded Lisa.

Kaz ignored her friend as her expression jumped from

relish at the gossip to concern over safety and back again. 'And I haven't finished my Christmas shopping yet,' she finished.

'Nor have I,' Lisa sighed. 'I still need something for my dad and brother. Why are men so difficult to buy for?'

'Don't change the subject,' Kaz objected.

'Don't the victims usually disappear when alone? Walking home from work or nightclubs?' Lisa asked. Her friend nodded. 'So, stick with the crowd when you're out, and don't be tempted by anyone unfamiliar. You'll be alright. He doesn't seem to target the shopping centre so, if you'll give me a minute, I'll go and get ready.' She slid from the stool.

'Don't be so cynical.'

'I'm not intending to be. We'll be together, and you can treat me to breakfast in that new place on the way in. Call it recompense for getting me up early after the staff do.'

'Oh, Raguel. I have found the perfect mate for you. You'll love her. She's not of colour, as they say today, but she is beautiful. In fact, she's very pale with white-blonde hair and intense blue eyes. She is a flawless contrast. You'll be Yin and Yang personified.

'What was that you said? Her name? Miniel. Her name is Miniel. Isn't that amazing? She will induce love in you, I am sure of it. I'll arrange a dinner where you can meet. I'm convinced you will not be alone for much longer. No more coveting other couples.'

Raguel smiles sheepishly but he knows I am right.

I hear a voice and turn right round. 'Yes, yes, my friend,' I answer her query. 'I shall find myself a wife once you are all settled. In fact, I have someone in mind.' I listen and insist. 'Oh, but I do. I'm not just saying that.'

I become uncomfortable when my own life comes under scrutiny. Mother has such an out-dated attitude and can be so nasty about my choice of associates. I have chosen my friends carefully but am still afraid they might judge as she does, so I change the subject. 'I've brought salmon today. I thought I would poach it with butter and fennel. You all like that. Asparagus is so expensive, it being December, but I've brought a few spears as a treat. It won't take long. Make yourselves comfortable at the table. Help yourselves to wine.'

I potter about preparing food, pouring cold, white wine, and generally conversing with my friends around the table. We do not chat inanely; we converse, engage in discourse and debate. Our discussions are deep and meaningful. We learn and express well-informed opinions without fear of repercussions.

They are anxious to hear about Miniel, and I take pleasure in describing her attributes, but Raguel must wait until after the Christmas period before meeting her. It's not that any of us are particularly religious, but Miniel tells me that she is going to stay with relatives until the New Year. A wedding will brighten the dark, cold days of January.

Raguel asks me to help him choose a suit for the occasion. I am so touched. I thought he might ask one of our other friends - but he wants me. I can hardly wait.

January

Lisa left the door ajar for her friend, who still gave a cursory tap before barging in. 'Have you heard the news?'

Kaz said sounding close to tears. 'It's Anni. You remember her, don't you?' Lisa had and did and the fact that someone they knew was missing had sobered her up somewhat regarding what the police were now referring to as possible murders due to some new evidence. Kaz dropped onto the settee and picked up the remote control for the television.

'We don't know she's been murdered, do we? Not really. She's just missing,' Lisa pleaded as Kaz found the news channel. 'The police aren't saying much, are they?'

The two friends had attended university with Anneli, who was Finnish and had come to England to study. They had been friends of sorts, not close but on speaking terms and had lost touch after graduation. 'Didn't she go out with Toby Walsh?' Lisa asked. 'I really fancied him at one time.'

'She married him,' Kaz stated. 'Only a few weeks ago, actually. It was in the local paper. Didn't you see the photo? They looked fabulous. Honeymoon in the Seychelles, lucky bastards.'

'I always wanted to look like her,' Lisa sighed. 'Legs up to her ears and flawless skin that tans as soon as the sun shows its face.'

'She's nice.'

'I know. Good looks and a lovely person. Life's a bitch.' It was meant as a joke, but neither was in the mood to laugh.

'Shh, shh. It's Toby.' Kaz turned up the sound. 'He looks just as gorgeous as he used to.' He looked washed out and scared to death to Lisa, but she had to admit her friend was right.

His in-laws, Mr and Mrs Nieminen, had flown over to

be close to the investigation and made the usual plea for the missing to come home, that they loved her dearly and if someone did know anything to let them or the police know because the pain was unbearable. Mrs Nieminen started to cry, and her husband hugged her. Toby sat forlorn and alone at the end of the table. The friends watched for a little longer, but when the story changed, Lisa turned the sound down.

'What did she do after uni, do you know?' she asked Kaz, who always seemed to know everything.

'She went to work for some charity, I think. She was always big on that sort of thing. Toby's a fully-fledged accountant now, so she can please herself what she does.'

Lisa was about to say 'some people have all the luck' but stopped herself in time. Anneli was missing, dead, kidnapped or just plain fallen out with her husband. None of it was good news. She sighed.

Kaz changed the subject. 'What about you and Harry? How's that going? Anything to add?'

'No. To be honest I'm beginning to wonder about him?'

'Wonder what?'

'I do like him, but ...'

'But what ...?'

'He's a bit odd.'

'Besides not having a mobile or being on social media? How else do you mean odd?'

'I don't know how to put it. Perhaps it's the women going missing, but his behaviour's ...' Lisa searched for a word but finally continued with, '...odd for someone his age.'

'Perhaps he had an abused childhood. Have you

thought of that?' Kaz mused. She'd watched a documentary about it only the other night.

'He's not said anything.'

'Well, he wouldn't, would he? Hardly a conversation starter. What do you know about his family?'

'Only child. No living family he cares to stay in touch with.'

'There you are then.'

'There I am, where?'

'I don't know. I'm not a psychologist. I just thought …' Kaz stopped and considered how to go on.

In truth, Lisa had been rather enjoying her romance with Harry because that was what it was, an old-fashioned romance rather than an affair.

'You know his mother was into all this New Age stuff. Lived in that commune just outside of town. What was it called?' Lisa volunteered.

'Not the one on Raleigh's Farm?'

'That's the one.' Kaz sniffed when she heard that. Its reputation for drugs and strange practices was legend in the area when the girls were at school. Lisa carried on. 'I haven't told you, have I? His real name is Hariel.'

'What the …!'

'I know. Apparently his mum called him after her guardian angel. You can see why he calls himself Harry. Says he was bullied at school.'

'Well, there you are then. An upbringing like that. It would cause all sorts of problems. He was probably brought up on a diet of sacrificed virgins and kale.'

'Idiot,' Lisa retorted but it made her smile. What she didn't add was that he liked to call her Hope rather than her given name because he never thought he would be able to feel the way he did about anyone. He said she would be the Eve to his Adam when the time was right. It made her feel a bit uncomfortable. That was it, not exactly scared – but definitely uncomfortable.

'He's a bit reserved, really.'

'Probably scared he'd show his true face otherwise.' Kaz was dipping into a box of chocolates on the coffee table. 'Don't you miss sex?' she asked between mouthfuls of chocolate.

'Hey, Harry bought me those.' Lisa took the box from her. 'They're expensive.'

'I know. They're delicious. You didn't answer. Again, do you miss sex?'

'If you must know …' Lisa realised she was playing with the gold locket he had bought her for Christmas and let it go instantly. He always seemed to have plenty of money, but the job couldn't pay that well.

'I knew it. I knew it. Perhaps he's waiting. Keeping himself pure.' Lisa laughed at Kaz's remark. 'Perhaps he'll propose on Valentine's Day. It's only two or three weeks away,' she added. She looked at her friend, the grin slowly fading from her face. 'You're very quiet. You wouldn't say yes?'

'No! I don't know. It's strange having a man who's not pushing for sex all the time.'

It was Kaz's turn to laugh. 'A modern man, good for him.'

As to Harry, at first Lisa had been flattered by his behaviour, but they'd been seeing each other for nearly seven weeks now and he'd not instigated anything and shied away if she made any sort of move. When she really made herself think about it, she still knew very little about him. At least, he'd not asked to borrow money.

'Well, here she is. Isn't she as lovely as I said she was? Come, come Miniel, don't be shy. There's a seat by Raguel. He's the gorgeous young man with the ebony skin. There, don't they look a treat? Ebony and Ivory. I might call you that. Just for tonight. If you've no objection, of course?'

I have no wish to be considered unPC. Is that even a word?

They don't object. My friends are easy going. They don't take offence at trivial remarks said in all honesty and without malice aforethought. Nor do they find deeper meaning in simple compliments like some I know.

I have prepared a special supper tonight in honour of Miniel's arrival. We are having pea soup to start, then fish pie with a beetroot salad, and apple donuts for dessert. I open a sparkling white wine, which compliments the sparkle in her eyes. This gesture makes everyone laugh and the ice is broken.

Miniel is wearing the beautifully styled red dress and jacket she was wearing when I first met her. It was the sight of her in that dress that made me think that she would make the perfect bride for Raguel. Apart from me, he is the only single person in our group. They are getting on so well I just know that they will become inseparable before very long.

Don't feel sorry for me. I have my eye on someone. We met recently but I have yet to show my feelings. I am very apprehensive and need to be certain. Mother drilled that into me from when I was quite young. 'Never make a move without being certain. Move in haste; repent in leisure,' she would say. 'If I hadn't opened my legs to your father, I would never have been saddled with you.' The men in our family are called after angels but I am always her "Little Jonah", but I know she loves me or why would she take the trouble to instil her values into me?

February

Kaz sipped her wine so daintily that Lisa began to wonder what she really wanted. She usually gulped the first glass down as if she was afraid it would evaporate before she had a chance to drink it.

'Still no developments I take it?' Kaz asked slyly. Lisa didn't bother answering. 'Does the arrangement suit you?'

'It's just that I feel safe when I'm with him,' Lisa replied. 'Not likely to be picked up by your friendly, local serial killer.'

'What do you do when you do meet?' Kaz put her wine glass down and Lisa knew she was in for the third degree.

'We have meals, go to the pub, see a film. Go to Maisie's.'

'I didn't have him down as a nightclub sort.'

'Well, he is. We do the usual things like any normal couple.' Lisa was being defensive and knew it, but couldn't help herself.

'Weird,' Kaz commented.

'Talking of weird, he often asks after Luke.'

'What's your brother got to do with anything?' Kaz asked and Lisa shrugged. 'Dump him, Lees. I'll organise a foursome with one of Jordan's mates.' Kaz was probably a reincarnated matchmaker from some ancient culture. She was happy with her Jordan and hated to see anyone on their own.

'I'll leave it until after Valentine's Day. I'll see what happens then.' Kaz's remark about him waiting for a romantic occasion had firmly settled in Lisa's subconscious.

'So, you're seeing him then?'

'Oh yes. That's a firm date. He said he's booked a table at Gino's, that Italian place in town.'

'The expensive one?'

'That's the one. It's only a week away. I've bought him a pressie.' Lisa got up and found her handbag. She rummaged around inside it until she found what she wanted.

'What on earth have you got him?' Kaz wanted to know. 'I wouldn't know where to start.'

'I know it's a bit soppy, but I like it.' Lisa passed a jewellery box to her friend who opened it and peeked inside.

'Oh, you are not wrong. I didn't take him as that sort of person.' Kaz held up a gold tie-pin adorned with a heart-shaped red stone. 'How much did that cost?'

'Not as much as you think. It's a garnet.'

'Are you really that serious? I thought you were just casual dating.'

'Do you think it's too much? Too soppy?'

'It'll be okay,' Kaz reassured her. 'There are worse things out there. It is Valentine's – soppy is king – or queen. Keep me informed, though. You know how I hate to be the last to know anything.' Lisa threw a cushion at her and they started to giggle. 'Did you say you'd got another bottle of wine in the fridge?' Lisa nodded. 'Fetch then while I put a film on.'

'Okay. And we can finish those chocolates he bought me,' Lisa decided.

Kaz selected *Ghost* on the film channel, an oldie but a goodie. They drank wine, ate chocolate, and wept.

I know I considered a January wedding but now I think we'll have it on St Valentine's Day; it's the perfect date. That's if Raguel and Miniel agree. It's not as if they have family to please. I can put on a feast. I shall enjoy that. It's been a long time since I made a special banquet for my friends.

Perhaps she could marry in the red dress? It so becomes her white skin. Ladies like their finery, though. It's just so difficult – a man shopping for a wedding dress on his own. Maybe she could borrow one from one of the other wives? Something borrowed? It will bring good luck. I'll tell her so.

Raguel and I have chosen a suit for him. It fits so well. I could marry him myself if we were so inclined. Mother would never approve.

A wedding on St Valentine's Day will mean cancelling a long-standing engagement, but that can't be helped. It would be nice to invite my significant other – how I love saying that – to the wedding but it's too soon. We have not been together long enough yet to be so familiar. Once this wedding is over, we'll have time for each other. Then, with luck, it will be my turn to be married and our little group will be complete.

February 14th

Kaz was lucky enough to have Valentine's Day off, so the girls had arranged to meet for coffee after Lisa finished her shift. 'So, what are you wearing tonight?' Kaz asked, and Lisa could feel her friend stare at her over her enormous cappuccino bowl as she stirred her coffee.

'We're not going now.' Lisa looked out of the window. Anything to avoid eye contact.

'What? It's Valentine's. I thought you were going to that Italian? Wait a minute.' Kaz's face broke into one enormous smile. 'Don't tell me you're having a night in?' Her expression told her friend what she was thinking.

'No. No night in. No night out. He's cried off. Cancelled the restaurant booking. He's not coming round. Nothing,' Lisa snapped.

'But it's Valentine's,' wailed Kaz.

'I know but it can't be helped.'

'Why ever not? What's his excuse? It had better be good. Someone had better be dying. He'd better be dying.'

'He says something urgent's come up. He's got to go and deal with it.'

'Perhaps he's married, and his missus won't let him go play.'

'He's not married,' Lisa replied tiredly. She was pissed with him if the truth be told. Pissed that she had to explain him to her friends.

'You know that for sure?'

'Of course,' Lisa retorted peevishly, but actually she didn't and that made her all the more irritable. She decided she'd definitely dump him when she next saw him – unless he had a really good excuse like the dog dying. Only, he hadn't got a dog.

'Oh, Lees. Finish with him. It's too late for tonight, I know, but I will arrange a foursome with one of Jordan's mates. Promise.'

Lisa nodded because it was easier than arguing and she didn't trust herself to speak. She might be angry enough to dump Harry, but nobody liked to be let down. She decided to buy herself some expensive bubble bath, order a takeaway and find a weepie on the movie channel. There was a bottle of Prosecco in the fridge. She had bought it – in case.

The girls went their separate ways: Lisa to wallow in self-pity and Kaz to make herself glamourous for her date with Jordan.

Lisa ran the water deep and hot, pouring in a copious amount of fragrant bubble bath. She also made sure she had the biggest glass of Prosecco and bugger the headache in the morning. At least it was a Friday, she could have a lie in in the morning.

Lisa was almost asleep when her phone trilled softly by her ear. She nearly missed the call, being disorientated by the wine and over-heated bath water, but just managed to catch it as it went to message. She hoped against hope that it was Harry, in the call box on the corner of her street. It wasn't. It was her brother's girlfriend.

'Hi, Em. Is everything alright?' she questioned.

'Is Luke with you?' Emily asked. There were no pleasantries.

'No. I presumed he would be with you it being Valentine's.' Lisa reached round for her glass of wine.

'He hasn't turned up. The restaurant is getting a bit

twitchy because they could have filled the table three times over tonight. You don't know where he is, do you?'

'Have you tried his mobile?' Daft question.

'Of course,' she answered shortly. 'It goes straight to answer. It's not like him.'

She was right. It wasn't like him. Lisa thought that he and Emily were sound. He'd even talked about asking her to set up home with him in a place of their own. Wanted to know his big sister's opinion.

'Could you pop round and see if he's in his flat? I don't want to leave in case he turns up late. I don't have his flatmate's new number. Have you?'

Max was forever changing his phone. 'Sorry, no. I will check for you, but I'm in the bath. I'll speak with Mum first. See if she knows anything. I'll get there as soon as I can get dressed.'

'Aw, sorry. You must be getting ready for your date.'

'No worries. He'll understand.' Lisa crossed her fingers at the lie.

Luke was not at their mum and dad's so that meant she had to get out of the bath, get properly dressed – in clothes – in order to go see her daft brother. She kept hoping Emily would ring to say he'd arrived, but she didn't. Lisa tried ringing her back, but the phone was engaged, and Luke didn't answer when she tried his again. Her mother rang her back. Now she'd worried her parents.

Local regeneration had cleared the rows of Victorian terraces and thrown up an array of low-rise apartments. Luke's flat was in a similar block to his sister's, three streets away so fortunately she didn't need to drive. She felt, not exactly drunk but, decidedly flushed with the wine she had consumed. There was a light on in the flat, and she cursed him roundly. If he couldn't make the date for whatever reason, he could at least have phoned Emily. No one spoke when Lisa pressed the button to her brother's flat, but a buzz indicated that the door was open. Luke's flatmate, Max, answered her knock.

'If you're after Luke, he left over an hour ago.'

'Left? For where?'

'His date with Emily. Duh.'

'He hasn't got there. Emily is livid.'

'Well, he got himself all glammed up and went out stinking of that aftershave she bought him for his birthday. Told me he was going to that new place on the High Street with – let me see? Oh, Emily.'

'Don't be funny. It doesn't suit you,' Lisa told him irritably. 'Plus, he never turned up. It doesn't take an hour to walk there from here.' She presumed he had walked in order for him to be able to have a drink.

'Have you phoned him?'

'Of course. We both have.'

Max dug into his dressing gown pocket and pulled out his mobile phone. 'It goes straight to answer.' He looked at the screen as if it was lying to him. 'Ring Emily. See if he's arrived yet.'

Emily answered this time. 'I'm outside – someone's letting me in. Is he there?'

They waited for her by the lift. 'Where is he?' Her bottom lip quivered, and Lisa had to swallow hard. Something was not right. This was so unlike her brother.

Oh, dear friends, I have so much to tell you. I'm afraid I've been keeping this from you until I was sure, but I have met the most wonderful person. I really think this is the one. He is the most handsome of men, and for me it was love at first sight. See, I knew you'd be happy for me. You are all such wonderful friends. Not a bit like mother. She will not approve. She likes life to have Adam with his Eve.

I've known for some time, but wasn't sure how he felt about me. Well, now I do know. He feels the same. He hasn't told me yet because he's shy, but I know it here, in my heart. Name? His name is Jophiel. It means "Beauty of God" and suits him so well. He is beautiful, both to look at and by nature. Don't I always choose the most perfect of people?

I haven't brought him to meet you today as I just want to get used to the idea of us being together. See what a jealous old thing I am. I'm afraid you'll fall in love with him yourselves. Don't look like that. I know you are as happy with a man as a woman or you wouldn't be here. I have told him about you, and he's dying to meet you. As soon as he is ready, I'll cook a special meal and introduce him to you all. We'll all get on famously, I'm sure.

February 15th

He was beyond confused. He couldn't understand where he was, what he was supposed to be doing or why he was there. Slowly he glanced around. His head was hurting like hell, his mouth dry, his eyes aching. For a minute he had to ask himself who he was. He was Luke, Luke Martin. The last thing he remembered was his flat. He was getting ready to go out, to celebrate some occasion with his girlfriend. He shouldn't be in this dark place. He was sitting in a chair with arms. He knew that because his arms were strapped to them. He also knew there was a name for the type of chair, but he couldn't think of it. The need to know the name for the type of chair began to fill his thoughts. Better that than why he was tied to a chair with arms, a chair whose style-name he couldn't remember, in a dark place. Better than dwelling on the fear that was threatening to overwhelm him.

He was working his mouth trying to induce some saliva when he heard a noise. Someone was coming. Luke wasn't convinced this was a good thing, but at least it might give him the answers to some of his questions. One had been answered already. Whoever was coming was walking down steps which, together with the dark and cool musty feeling, meant he must be in a cellar of sorts.

The light the newcomer switched on was not bright, but it still hurt his eyes. He closed them quickly and then carefully squinted through his lashes. He wished he hadn't tried to open them again. He supposed he had been expecting to see a man. Why it should have been a man didn't enter his head. It could just as easily have been a female who tied you up in a dark cellar, this being the twenty-first century.

He wasn't sure who was in front of him. Slim, medium height for a man, tallish for a woman. This person had no face. At least it must have but it was obscured by a mask: hard and white with painted features, and black holes for eyes. The hair was short, black, sharply cut and framed the face. Whoever it was just stood there silently watching.

Luke opened his mouth to speak but could only croak due to the dryness of his throat. The creature leant forward and raised an arm, and he could not help but flinch as the gloved fingers gently stroked his cheek.

'Shh my sweet. Everything will be fine once you're settled. But first I think we'd better get you dressed.' The voice was distorted through the mask. There was nothing at all for Luke to identify this person by.

It was easy – easier than I expected. He was so grateful when I offered him a lift into town that he never asked why I was outside his block of flats. He didn't flinch when I offered him my hipflask. So trusting. I know he is the right one because of that. Even so, I used a little of my stash of drugs just to keep him calm. I have no wish to hurt him. Some of my friends have been a little upset when I've introduced them to the others. I'm afraid they have put up a bit of a fight. Of course, they are fine once they get to know them and I'm sure he will be too, but I wish to proceed with care. I would not hurt him for the world.

February 18th

'No sign?' Kaz looked worried as she plonked herself down next to her friend's workstation. It was Tuesday morning. The rota had scheduled Lisa off on the Monday, but she hadn't enjoyed it. She had spent the day at her parent's home until her older sister, Lottie, had arrived. Both Lottie and their mother burst into tears and the anxiety level then spiralled to the point that Lisa excused herself by saying she was going to try Luke's friends again. She spent the rest of the day trying Luke's mobile to no avail. It now appeared to be off or out of battery.

Kaz was waiting. 'No,' Lisa told her.

'Should you be here?' Kaz looked concerned.

'What else can I do? I don't want to be at home on my own.' Lisa fiddled for a tissue and Kaz passed her one from her pocket. It was a bit runkled but clean.

'You could go to your mum and dad's,' Kaz offered.

'No thank you. I had enough yesterday. Lottie's with them, anyway. They're in bits. I just couldn't stand all that tea drinking and neighbours dropping in.'

'Is your sister staying?'

'She says she will – for a few days. She's better at this emotional support thingy than me. Her mother-in-law's looking after the girls for her. She's as anxious as the rest of us,' Lisa hiccupped.

'What about the police?'

'He's a healthy adult. They'll keep a look out, but he's not a priority. Not yet anyway.'

'The bloody hell, Lees. What are you supposed to do?'

'They put us in touch with a missing persons charity. As if that will do any good.'

'Have you told them this is out of character?'

'Of course,' she retorted. 'It didn't make a scrap of difference.'

'They didn't say that about Anni.'

'Well they wouldn't, would they? Not with the two women missing. They picked it up quicker than they would normally.'

'What about Harry? What does he say?' Kaz wanted to know.

Lisa shook her head. 'I can't get hold of him as he still hasn't a phone. Do you think he's in yet?'

'Haven't a clue. He might be if he's on the rota. Go upstairs. Ask Glenda if you can use the office phone to speak to orthopaedics and find out,' Kaz urged. 'It'll be more private than here.'

Lisa nodded but didn't move. 'I can't even think where Luke might be. None of his friends have seen him. His phone is off or dead. Oh, Kaz. You hear of these things, but never think it could happen to you. What if the killer's got him?'

'Well, he usually goes for women – or has done up to now,' Kaz reassured her. 'Your Luke is quite a bit of eye candy, let's face it. Perhaps he does have another girlfriend and is scared of telling Em.'

'Don't be an idiot. He loves Emily, but even if he did have another girl, he wouldn't be so daft as to just disappear from the face of the earth,' Lisa hoped.

'I suppose.'

'He'd let me, or Mum, know.'

'What's up, you two? Not planning on working today?' The girls were so wrapped up in their concerns that they hadn't heard anyone approach.

'Sorry, Lynne, but Lisa's brother Luke's gone missing and the police won't do anything,' Kaz snapped at their line manager.

'Your Luke's a big boy. Perhaps he found himself a warm bed somewhere.' Most women with a pulse fancied Luke.

'He was going to ask Emily to move in with him on Valentine's, but he didn't turn up.'

'That was Friday.' Lynne sounded a bit more concerned.

'He's been missing all weekend. He hasn't turned up for work at all, and none of his friends know where he is.'

'Aw, Lees,' Lynne sympathised. 'Should you be here?'

Kaz answered for her. 'She doesn't want to be home alone and can't face her mum's neighbours.'

'Go take her for a coffee, Kaz.'

'She wants to phone Harry,' Kaz told her.

'Harry?' Lynne sounded puzzled.

'Yes, Harry from orthopaedics. What's his surname, Lees?' Kaz turned to her friend.

'I've not heard of any Harry in orthopaedics.' Lynne looked puzzled. 'Why do you want to speak to him anyway?'

'I'm going out with him,' Lisa snuffled. 'Well, seeing him sometimes. He told me he worked there. He was at the Christmas do. Smartly dressed, good looking?' She was beginning to sound hysterical.

'Haven't you rung him? Found out what's going on?'

'He hasn't a phone.'

'He hasn't got a phone? How come? Everyone's got a phone.' Lynne sounded incredulous.

'Has anyone called Harry ever worked there?' Kaz was suspicious.

'I don't know. I know we're a small hospital, but I don't know everyone who works in every department.' Lynne became embarrassed. She liked a chat, but she was professional and didn't usually gossip. 'Haven't you got *any* contact details? A surname?' Lynne was beginning to sound suspicious now.

'He's being all dark and mysterious,' Kaz informed her. 'Fair and mysterious, I should say.'

'Well, there's mysterious and downright underhand,' sniffed Lynne.

'Kaz is being ridiculous. She thinks I'm daft for sticking with him.' Lisa was getting more upset.

'Well, it is a bit unusual. What do you know about him, Lees?'

Lisa suddenly realised she really did know nothing about him. What she did know was all surface stuff that anyone could find out. 'Not much if the truth be known,' she finally admitted, and not just to Lynne but to herself.

'You should be careful. Especially as women are going missing.'

Lisa got up shakily. 'I think I will have a word with the office. Perhaps Glenda can tell me more. Perhaps he used to work here.' She was grasping at straws. 'Glenda should be able to look him up anyway.'

'As you like, Lees, but remember we're all here for you.' Lynne patted her colleague's back in what she considered was a comforting manner as she made her way to the offices.

As Lisa opened the door to Glenda's office the secretary looked up with the phone in her hand. Two strangers were standing by her desk.

'Oh, Lisa, I was just about to ring you. The police are here. They want a word.'

Jophiel is proving to be a tad uncooperative. I had thought that we might enjoy each other's company before I introduce him to my friends, but he doesn't seem as interested in me as I thought he was. I know he has a girlfriend, but I thought that was just cover. I mean, I have a girlfriend too, but it doesn't mean anything. It's just to keep Mother quiet.

I have had to use all manner of inducements to keep him receptive to my needs. He rattles the chair so hard that I've had to secure it further. Mother will hear him if I'm not careful and then the waste will hit the fan as they say. I had hoped that I could have taken a week from work in order for us to get to know each other intimately, but they said I'd used up my allocation for this year and I was not allowed. I am related to the bosses; you would think I could have some perks.

I think I shall have to move more quickly than I anticipated. I was so looking forward to the week in just his company before sharing him.

Jophiel will insist on pushing against his bonds, despite me explaining to him that they are bonds of affection. He says they hurt him, but they are made of silk and love. I would not hurt him for the world. If he just calmed down and stopped resisting, I could release him. It is for his own good that he is secure in my special place. He needs time to realise that he loves me as much as I love him. I have made it as comfortable as I can for him. He has everything he needs, and I have offered nourishing food and drink to keep him healthy. He didn't like the clothes I have picked out for him, and I needed to give him something to calm him down before I could induce him to wear them.

I very nearly broke my vow and tasted him while he was sleeping. As it was, I ran my fingers over his flawless body, but I went no further this time. I want everything to be perfect. He would never have known but I would and that would have been a secret from him, and I want no secrets. Once he accepts me, he will be able to taste the delights I have for him.

He seemed to enjoy our friendship previously. I don't know what's up with him now.

'I'm sorry. Could you repeat that? I don't know what you're talking about.' Lisa was in shock to say the least.

'Why didn't you tell us your brother knew Anneli Walsh?' It was the man who asked. He had introduced himself as DI something or another. Lisa had been expecting bad news and was too frightened and upset for anything to sink in. Glenda had made her excuses and they were sitting in her office.

'He doesn't as far as I'm aware. I knew her at uni, but we weren't special friends. We drifted apart when we left.'

'And you didn't talk about her with your brother? When she went missing?' The other detective sounded kind.

'No. Luke and I don't see too much of each other. He has his life. I have mine.'

'He never mentioned her, at all?' She was all smiles, but they didn't reach her eyes.

'Why should he?'

'You tell me?' the first detective chipped in.

'I really don't know what to say. He doesn't know her.'

'As far as you are aware?'

'What? You think they had a "thing" going and have run away together?' Lisa snapped at him. 'You're mad if you do.'

The detective didn't turn a hair. The second detective, still smiling, answered the question with another. It was becoming annoying. 'Is it likely?'

'No. He has his own girlfriend. He was going to ask her to move in with him.'

'That would be one Emily Jones.' The first detective consulted his notebook. It was like something from the telly. Lisa nearly laughed but knew if she did it would turn to tears.

'Yes,' she said instead.

'She knows Anneli Walsh.' Was it a statement or a question? She couldn't be sure anymore.

'I imagine a lot of people know Anneli.' Lisa was losing the fear she felt when told the police wanted to see her, and was getting annoyed with them. She knew her brother. He wouldn't hurt another person. She sighed, 'Not as far as I know, but I could be wrong. I don't know *all* of Emily's friends. We are just normal people living normal lives. You never imagine that you would have to justify your every move.'

They waited for her to finish. 'What do you know about the money that has gone missing?'

'Money? Missing? How much money? Where from?'

'Quite a lot, actually. From Farrington, Farrington & Farrington, the firm your brother works for. Small amounts have been moved over time, but it only came to light after he disappeared.'

Lisa didn't know what to say. She was too agitated to take in anything else they said, and eventually they must have realised they would get nothing useful from her. She stumbled downstairs to where Lynne and Kaz were waiting impatiently.

Lisa stared at Lynne. 'Can I go home?' She burst into tears.

Kaz took her home in her car and a flurry of promises to keep Lynne informed as soon as she knew anything.

Once in Lisa's flat, Kaz pushed a glass of whisky into her friend's hand as she waited for the kettle to boil. She hadn't said anything, asked anything. She was a true friend and waited until Lisa was steady enough to tell her all she knew.

Lisa took a large gulp of the whisky, but was too

agitated to sit, and stalked around the flat tapping the glass and looking anxiously at her friend. Eventually she felt able to tell Kaz what the police had said.

'They have implied that he knows Anneli and that he has embezzled enough money from the firm in order that they can run away together.'

That rocked Kaz to the core. 'You're having a giraffe?'

'That they have, in fact, run away together with the missing money,' Lisa reiterated. Kaz poured herself a whisky.

'They cannot be serious? Luke? And Anneli? Come off it, what did they really say?'

'That thousands of pounds, Luke and Anneli have all gone missing at the same time. They've added it all together …'

'And got the wrong answer,' sighed Kaz. 'Luke doesn't know Anni. Does he?'

'Not that I'm aware of, but apparently she did approach the firm for sponsorship for one of her charities. She visited the premises on a number of occasions around Christmas.'

'Would Luke have seen her? Had anything to do with her?'

'I haven't a clue. Her poor family. Whatever must they be thinking?'

'I dread to think. The trolls will be out once this gets round.' Kaz checked her phone. 'But not yet.'

'I tell you what, let's talk to Em. See if she knows anything about this.'

'Good idea. Give her a bell, see if she's in. This will be better face to face. I'll drive. I've only had a sip of my drink.'

Emily had given up on work for the foreseeable future and had called in sick. She was at the door waiting for them when they arrived. The police had been to see her immediately after they came to see Lisa. She had been crying and looked dreadful. She started to cry again as the friends ushered her inside. Kaz put her kettle on and they settled in the kitchen. 'He wouldn't,' Emily managed to whisper.

'We know that,' Kaz retorted, 'that's why we've come to see you. We're going to do our own investigating.'

Lisa looked at her nervously. 'Are we?'

'Too right.' Kaz could be a tad overzealous when she got an idea, and things had gone awry quite spectacularly in the past. 'The police have obviously got set ideas and will be barking up the wrong tree. It's up to us to get evidence to prove them wrong and set them on the right course.' She plonked two cups of coffee on the kitchen table. 'Okay. One: does Luke know Anneli?' She turned to pick up her own drink.

Emily shook her head emphatically. 'Neither of us knows Anneli. He mentioned that she had approached the office for sponsorship but only after we saw that she was missing on the news.'

'What did he say, exactly?' Kaz rummaged in her bag for paper and pen. She came up with an old envelope and a broken ballpoint.

'Oh, I can't remember *exactly*. We were watching the news and the piece came on and Luke said something like, "I know of her. She came to see Gabriel the other day."'

'Gabriel?' Kaz looked from one to the other.

'One of the partners,' Lisa offered. 'Of course, she

wouldn't see Luke. He's only a paralegal. She's bound to have liaised with one of the partners if she was after sponsorship.'

'Would Luke have seen her about?' Kaz asked.

'He might have done.' Emily considered for a minute. 'He never said. He can't talk much about work. It's all confidential'

'Was there anything different in his behaviour? You know – to make you wonder if anything was up?' Kaz continued her interrogation.

'Such as?' Emily asked.

'I don't know. He's your man. Was he different leading up to his disappearance?'

'No.'

Her friend sighed theatrically in exasperation. 'Come on, Em. Help us out here.'

'I would if I could, but Luke was no different leading up to his disappearance. It was all so sudden.' She was on the verge of tears again.

'Perhaps we're going the wrong way about this,' Lisa offered. 'Perhaps we should be talking to his work colleagues.'

'Chat to this Gabriel?' Kaz asked.

'Oh, you don't chat to the Brothers. Not without an appointment,' warned Emily as Lisa shook her head. Kaz really had no idea how things worked.

'Brothers? I thought they were partners?'

'Both,' Emily and Lisa said together. Lisa nodded to Emily.

'The Farrington brothers are partners in the firm,' she began. 'There are three brothers. Michael is the eldest and mostly retired now, although I believe he does a few hours for old clients.'

'Go on,' Kaz urged, pre-empting a change of direction.

'There seems to be quite a gap in ages, but Raphael is now the senior partner in his brother's stead and Gabriel the junior although they must both be in their sixties.'

'Married?' asked Kaz.

'Yes. Well, the younger two are. I think Michael's a widower but nothing untoward as far as I know,' Emily finished.

'Who else works there?' Kaz wanted to know.

'Well, there's Mrs Evans, the secretary. She's been there for ever. There's a couple of younger secretaries, mainly for typing and photocopying from what Luke says. Then there's the office gofer. They usually take a law student for work experience. I think it's a Kyle this time, or it could be Kylie, but I can't be sure. They seem to change so quickly. Two junior solicitors, a Marnie Leaman, and an Usman Pervez. Then there's Luke, who's a paralegal and Jon. I'm not exactly sure what Jon's role is, although Luke mentions him quite a bit.'

'What's his surname?' Kaz asked.

'I don't know. Luke has said but I can't remember. I think it begins with an F though.'

'We might be able to chat to this Jon Whatsisname – beginning with F I think,' Lisa suggested. 'Only, I'm not going anywhere near that office. If the Brothers think Luke has stolen the money, they'll not want to see me.'

'Do they know you?' Emily wanted to know.

'I've been to the office to meet up with Luke on

occasion. The Brothers are nice, grandfatherly sort of men. Everything's such a mess.' Lisa felt ready to cry but knew that it would not solve anything.

'I'll speak with this Jon if you like,' offered Kaz. 'I'm not quite so emotionally involved, for a start. No one there knows me. I could make an appointment with him.'

'I don't know about the appointment,' Emily wondered. 'For a start, we don't know what he does so we don't know what to say. If you dither about once in, he could make a fuss and then you'd be discovered and thrown out. We'd be really stuck then.'

'Right, if I can't make an appointment with him, I could just wait outside and try and waylay him. Do either of you know anything about him? Where he drinks? Hangs out?'

'Luke says he's a bit of a lone wolf. He's inclined to be standoffish, although he and Luke get on in a funny peculiar sort of way. I don't know anything about him really,' Emily mused. 'Only …'

'Yes?'

'I think he's related to the Brothers somewhere along the line. His name's not Farrington, though. I would have remembered that.'

'Okay, I'll just have to pick him up,' Kaz decided. 'Has he a girlfriend? I want to know how to play this.'

'Haven't a clue,' sighed Emily. 'Luke says he's mentioned a girl, but he thinks she's made up because the details change.' Her voice caught as she said his name. Kaz was not put off.

'What does he look like?'

'Average height, a bit shorter than Luke, but wiry and blondish,' Emily offered. 'Good looking. Very good looking from what Luke says, and always immaculate. Hates mess and clutter.'

'Sounds a bit like your Harry, Lees,' commented Kaz before continuing without giving her time to reply. 'Okay and what time would he knock off?'

'Well, that depends on what's going down, but it's usually around five.'

'Okay, I'll hang about outside the offices at five o'clock,' Kaz decided.

'There's a pub across the road,' Emily told her. 'You could say you were on your way there and meeting him was a coincidence.'

Lisa looked thoughtful. Something Kaz had said was bothering her. 'Aren't you worried?' she asked her.

'What about? Social media?' Kaz was obsessed with social media.

'I've turned that off and you should too. No, he could be the one taking these women.'

'Don't be a twonk. He works for a firm of solicitors and he knows Luke. He'll be sound.'

I'm sorry, I know I'm not good company tonight. Questions are being asked from a number of sources. Mother being the most insistent. She must have called the police because they have been to the house to question me about a missing man. I know she's only looking out for me as she's got it into her head I'll be next. It is so embarrassing trying to explain her to the police. I had to pretend to be friendly with them and joke and laugh at her little peccadilloes. I couldn't get rid of them. All the while I was thinking that Jophiel might make a noise. I know I made it soundproof, but I still get paranoid.

Then, when I came down here to be with him and calm

down – well, he was so unkind. He tried to bite me – there I've admitted it. People say that the course of true love never runs smoothly, and I fear they are right. Jophiel has caused me such great concern that I have had to bring things forward for fear of losing him. I'm afraid I lost control. I didn't even give him any drugs to calm him down. He refused food at first, and although he's eating a little now, he was still weak enough for me to have my way with him. This is not what I wanted for us. I was hoping to wait until after the ceremony.

February 19th

'Excuse me, but are you Jon – Jon who works with Luke?' The young man in question looked around him as if Kaz might have been addressing someone behind him. 'I'm looking for Jon. I'm a friend of Luke's ...'

'I'm not interested.'

'Sorry? Not interested in what? I've not told you what I want.' Kaz took a step closer. They were in a shadowed part of the street, and he was muffled in hat and scarf against the biting February wind. She couldn't see him clearly, but she was aware that the young man seemed embarrassed at being addressed by her in front of the other office workers, and pushed it to her advantage.

'I just want to talk to you. How about a drink? Across the road? That pub looks okay.'

'I'm not like that. I'm not interested. Go away.'

'I just want to ask about Luke. Nothing else.' Kaz continued to step forwards, pushing her luck gently. She heard someone snigger and watched the young man continue to fluster. 'Please. It won't take long.' Another step.

'Okay,' he snapped. 'Just not here. Or there.' A nod of his head indicated the pub. 'My car's just up here.' Kaz took a step back and the man seemed to relax. 'I live with my mother. She'll be expecting me – for tea.' His fingers were hard and tight around her wrist. How had he done that? She hadn't seen him move. 'Join us for a cup of tea and we can talk. Mother doesn't get many visitors.'

She thought he had put his hand into his pocket for his car keys, but she was wrong. Whatever he sprayed towards her face knocked her for six.

A man was changing the menu board outside the pub. He seemed more interested in them than what he was doing, and she wanted to call out but found she couldn't. She could do nothing to prevent Jon from helping her into the car before everything went dark.

As if things couldn't get any worse, I was picked up by a street girl on my way from the office today. It wasn't even late at night. I told her that I was not interested, but she was very insistent, said she knew Luke. I didn't think he was like that. It was so embarrassing. Everyone was looking at us as they left the office. I just panicked and pretended I knew her. They were all sniggering and giving sideways glances. I know I shall be the subject of gossip, but it can't be helped. I thought of taking her home, but Mother would have something to say about that, so I've had to bring her here. She won't bother you; she's in the next room. I do hope you don't mind. I know you won't, you're such good friends. I shall get rid of her as soon as I can.

I can still feel my heart pounding. I don't know what to

do. I can't cook. Everything will go wrong; I know that for sure. I couldn't eat anyway. Perhaps it would be for the best if we postponed tonight. You go, dear friends, and I'll deal with this girl. Tomorrow will be different. Everything will be back to normal. Don't you worry about me, I can manage.

It was getting late and there had been no word from Kaz. Lisa was beginning to get jittery. She'd tried her friend's mobile, but it went straight to answer. She tried Emily, but she had heard nothing either. Lisa would have liked to have gone to join her but was too scared to go out by herself, so opened her laptop and they chatted over Skype. It was reassuring to see a friendly face. Emily reminded her that Kaz was a big girl and could take care of herself, but Lisa wasn't so sure.

'Come on, Lees. Woe betide any man who tries to get the better of her. Do you remember that time she took her car to the garage because there was a funny noise?'

'Oh, yes,' Lisa laughed. 'She wiped the floor with the mechanic. I think he still has a nervous tick every time he sees a female.'

Lisa's phone ringing broke into the laughter which was beginning to turn to tears. 'It's Jordan,' she told Emily. 'I need to get this. Stay there. Hi Jordan. What's to do?' She put her phone on speaker as she and Emily were sharing everything.

'Is Kaz there? Only, we were supposed to be meeting tonight and I can't reach her.'

'Is she not with you?' Lisa had been hoping that that was the reason her friend hadn't been picking up her phone.

'Duh, no. That's why I'm ringing. And her phone goes

straight to answer. I know she can be flexible with her time-keeping but she's never usually this late.'

Lisa's stomach turned. She couldn't still be with that Jon. It was nearly nine o'clock. 'Let me speak to Emily,' she told him and cut him off. She didn't want him to hear what she'd got to say, not yet anyway.

'Did you hear that?' Emily nodded on screen.

'Do you think we should call the police?' she whispered.

They both knew they were going to look right idiots, but it couldn't be helped. 'I think so. We'll have to tell all,' Lisa warned her. 'They won't be happy with us.'

'I don't care. I'm really worried. What if she was picked up by the killer?'

'Okay. I'll do it. Then I'll get back to Jordan. It's the least I can do.'

The police weren't as helpful as Lisa thought they would be in the current climate of missing women, but when she explained who she was and what they'd done they said they would send someone round when they could.

I thought this would be a joyous time. I had scheduled my evenings to be alone with my new mate in order to get to know him and for him to know me. This girl has ruined everything. Jophiel is proving more difficult than I envisaged, and now she has butted in.

I am used to every aspect of my life being subject to meticulous planning, and this was not planned. I really don't know what to do. I cannot cope with surprises so I could have left all sorts of clues I am unaware of. I told my friends that everything will be alright tomorrow, but I am not so sure of that anymore.

I need to think but my head is spinning, and I can't find any solution. She's not the sort of person I would consider as a friend. Anyway, everyone here has a partner – every Adam his Eve. My table is balanced when my friends come round for a meal. She will spoil the symmetry. There's no room for more. We would be crowded and we can't have that.

When Kaz came to she found herself gagged and tied to a chair. There was no light, no draught and the musty damp air told her she was most likely in a cellar or a disused building. There was also a sharp tang of chemicals that reminded her of the hospital. She struggled but only succeeded in hurting herself, the rope chafing her wrists. What a mess. She felt nauseous from whatever he had sprayed her with and hoped that she wouldn't throw up inside her gag. At least she'd been seen with this Jon – she presumed he was Jon. His co-workers had seen them and the man from the pub. She relaxed but only slightly. She didn't know how long it would be before she was missed, it was so cold, and she needed a wee.

A noise made her jump. Her first thought was rats, but she soon realised that she could hear footsteps coming from another part of the cellar. A dim light made her squint, and she couldn't quite see who had come in. Her fear took quite another turn as she began to focus. Someone was watching her silently. She couldn't tell if it was male or female at first, but as her eyes travelled upwards she noticed the unmistakeable masculine shape of the body under the formless clothing. The face was covered in a mask, white with painted features, a perfectly sculptured black bob framing the face.

What was worse was the table spread with an array of surgical instruments standing between her and him. And he was dressed in scrubs.

She sits there silently glaring at me making me nervous. I want to get rid of her but have nothing ready with which to process her. I don't know what to do without it leading back to me, to my friends. I couldn't do that to them. I know we were seen by everyone from the office. They'll all be talking about it.

She really is superfluous to requirements, but I can't let her leave. She knows who I am and will tell the police. I'm sure she'll plead otherwise, but I know people. It'll just be a ploy for me to let her go. The police are already suspicious. It'll bring them straight back to me.

I need to come up with a plan so that people think she was elsewhere after we spoke, but I cannot think at the moment.

The police were not impressed with the girls. They seemed to imply that whatever happened it would probably be their own fault. Lisa had to explain everything, where Kaz was going and why. She tried to be a bit evasive in order to save face, but was so worried that she couldn't keep the story plausible, and ended up telling everything.

Jordan came around. He was livid. He phoned Kaz's parents and soon there was mayhem in Lisa's flat. While everyone was shouting and vying for space, Lisa's phone signalled a message. Everyone stopped talking and turned to her. Shaking, she looked at the screen.

'It's from Kaz,' she uttered. No one spoke as she opened the message. For a moment she didn't know what to say. She was glad the police were already there. 'She says she won't be dropping in tonight. She's going straight home.' Lisa looked pale. 'That's not Kaz. She didn't send this. It's not even text spelling and she wasn't coming here tonight.'

'No, she was coming to me,' Jordan told the police.

'She wouldn't say *home* either. She always said *the flat*. Home to her was her family home,' Lisa explained.

The atmosphere changed instantly, and the police took charge. Kaz lived in the same block as Lisa, so Mr and Mrs Bailey took the spare key Lisa kept and went to her flat with Jordan and a police officer. Emily wanted to come and sit with Lisa, but was advised to stay put. Lisa had to agree, even though she would have relished the friendly face.

'What on earth were you thinking?' It was the smiley police person, although she wasn't smiling now.

'Nobody would listen,' Lisa insisted. 'The money. The disappearing without a word. It's so out of character. You wouldn't listen. We thought we'd try and get some proof and bring it to you.'

'We will follow all avenues,' the woman stated.

'Oh yeah?' Lisa sniffed. 'Well, it didn't sound like you were planning to do so. You seemed to have got it all sown up.'

'There are a number of discrepancies we need to investigate,' she told her. Lisa pulled a disbelieving face.

'You must appreciate we cannot tell you everything in case it jeopardises the case.'

'Whatever.' Lisa no longer felt civil. She felt that if they'd done their job properly in the first place, they would not be in this mess. 'So, what happens now?'

'A cup of tea would be nice.' The police person tried to be friendly, but Lisa was having nothing of it. 'Just while we get your statement written up.'

Lisa pulled herself from her seat as if it was the greatest effort in the world and banged about in the kitchen area making tea. She started to realise that it was not actually the young woman's fault, so dug about in the cupboard for the packet of Jammie Dodgers she'd hidden in case of an emergency at the start of the post-Christmas diet. Today was a justifiable emergency.

As she tucked into tea and biscuits, the police person asked Lisa to call her Janine. While taking the statement, her walkie-talkie beeped annoyingly. She shrugged apologetically and moved away to answer it privately. The distance and tinny crackles made it hard for Lisa to understand what was being said. Eventually Janine returned to Lisa. 'She was seen getting into a car just after five. The landlord of the pub opposite remembers seeing her when he was changing his sign to the evening menu. She didn't look as if she wanted to go with the young man at first, so he watched to see if she needed assistance. What with the disappearances and all. Then she seemed to acquiesce, so he went back inside.' A sob-like noise escaped from Lisa as she listened to her. 'He didn't see which direction they left in, nor did he get the registration number, but he did get make and colour. We'll track them on the CCTV. Don't worry. We're on to it.' She finished her tea and took another biscuit. 'I just thought you should know.' Lisa nodded, unable to speak.

'Will you be alright?' Janine asked. 'Have you anyone who could stay?'

'I'll be fine.' Lisa cleared her throat. 'I'll go back on Skype and chat to my friend.'

'Okay. Don't hesitate to give us a ring if anything crops up. Anything at all.' She made for the door. 'And don't do anything silly.'

Lisa shut the door and locked it. Emily was also involved with the police, so she sat and stared into space. What had they done?

I can't believe I didn't think of this before. I've been getting myself in a state over nothing. Well, not exactly nothing but something easily remedied. I haven't been thinking straight.

Mother has been complaining for a long time now about the way she is left alone while I'm at work or entertaining my friends. Not that she knows about my friends. She thinks I work long hours and she keeps saying she'll have a word with my uncles. However, when I show her how much money I have she keeps her counsel. I told her that I had been made a partner in the firm and she was so delighted. She said that it was only my right. One day, though, she will carry out her threat, talk to my uncles and discover the truth: that I am no partner. I only took what money I felt was owed me because I should have been made a partner by right of birth. But how will that make me look in her eyes? The solution to this is to present her with a companion. This strange female will become her confidante and that will solve two problems in one go. A place for her and a companion for Mother. I wonder what her name is? I didn't even ask I was in such a panic. Mother will ask. She always wants to know everything.

I have to prepare this woman to meet Mother and that is going to take some work. I have nothing ready and she is quite a big girl. She panicked so when she saw my friends, so the start has been a bit messy. I have such a lot to do, I must get on. I don't want to spoil another day with this.

February 20th

'Ms Martin?' It was not the smiley police person at Lisa's door. It was the first detective, DI Clarke – she remembered his name now. He looked decidedly grim. Her heart sank and she felt lightheaded and grabbed for the door frame to steady herself. She managed to nod. 'Can we come in?' There were two of them, the other being a uniformed police person. Lisa stood aside and indicated that they were, if not welcome, at least allowed entry.

They sat, the detective on the settee and Lisa in the chair. The uniform perched at the breakfast bar and Lisa looked from one to the other expectantly.

'We have some news…' the Detective Inspector began.

'Luke or Kaz? Er, Katherine,' she asked.

'The investigation mainly,' he informed her. 'Do you know a Jonah Finnian? He works with your brother at Farrington's.'

'Would that be Jon Finnian? Luke has mentioned a Jon. I don't recall his surname.'

'Possibly. Did he talk about him at all? What he's like?'

'Not really. He might mention him in passing. We don't talk about work much. As I said, we have our own lives. From what Luke did say he sounds a bit – what you might call anal.'

'How do you mean – anal?'

'Pedantic. Inflexible. Has quaint ideas. Luke also said that he has no real friends that he knows of and everyone in the office laughs at him behind his back.'

'Quite a lot of information for people who don't talk much,' the Inspector responded wryly.

Lisa pulled a face and he carried on, 'But Luke was friendly with him?'

'Luke likes people. He's a friendly guy. It's his default setting. It sounded like they got on alright at work. I don't know. Socially Luke was either at the rugby club or with his girlfriend. You should speak to Emily. She might know more.'

'Someone will be.'

'Is this Jonah – Jon – a suspect?'

'Perhaps a cup of tea might be nice.' So, no real information was forthcoming. Lisa went to get up, but the detective turned to his colleague. 'Chris? Do the honours, please.' He looked around. 'Nice little flats, these.'

'Little being the operative word,' Lisa told him. 'But it's fine for the likes of me and Kaz. Affordable, you know.' What was he going to tell her? She could feel her heart beginning to race. 'We can be independent.'

He reached into a pocket and placed a small item in a plastic wallet on the coffee table. 'Do you recognise this?'

Lisa instinctively went to pick it up, but stopped as she

recognised it. It was a small diamond stud set for a pierced ear. 'It's Kaz's. Or at least one just like it. Her parents bought her the earrings and a pendant for her twenty-fifth birthday,' she told him. 'Where did you find it?'

'Would she have been wearing it when she went to meet with this friend of Luke's?'

'Yes. She wears them all the time. Please, tell me. What do you know?'

'Nothing concrete, at the moment. You must appreciate it would be silly of us to give you information that has not been verified.' She nodded. 'I'm sorry,' he said and picked up the packaged earring, hiding it safely. 'We will keep you informed when there is something to tell.' He rose to his feet and indicated to the uniform that she should leave the tea. They made for the door just as Lisa's phone started to ring. 'Get your phone,' he said. 'We'll see ourselves out.'

It was Emily. She had been asked the same questions as her friend, apart from the earring. She knew nothing about the earring. They were both very scared.

The police have been around again. They have been to the office a number of times, which I expected as that young lady from the charitable organisation who is missing had been there to see Gabriel. Now, they think Luke and she have vanished with all that money. That's fine; it will take the emphasis off me. I can cope with them at the office, but they have been to my home while I was at work and antagonised Mother. I don't know what they think they have on me as I've been very careful. I don't watch the news as a rule, but I've kept an eye on it since the incident with the lady of the night.

Nothing's been said that should worry me. Mother always thinks that there is no smoke without fire, so I shall be in for an interrogation to rival the Spanish Inquisition tonight. I can't even appease her with her new companion yet as she has not been processed. It takes time to do it properly and I dare not do a sloppy job. Mother will spot it. I can never do anything right by her; it doesn't matter how hard I try.

February 21st

Luke had been working at the chair from the minute he regained some sort of lucidity. It was sturdy but quite old. He remembered having some just like it in their dining room when he was growing up. They were all the rage then. His capturer had secured the legs to the floor after he heard him banging about, but that actually helped. He was able to pull against them and work the arms loose. Luke played rugby, he was fit and strong, and even though he took just enough food to keep himself going he was able to work at the chair until it was ready to fall apart.

He didn't know how much time he had. He knew the usual routine. He was left alone all day with his gaoler coming to see him morning and evening. The timing fitted with him going to work. If he had a job, then Luke had all day to attempt to free himself. When Luke thought of his captor he thought of work. Something was nagging at the back of his mind, but he couldn't bring it forward. The more he thought, the worse it became. He gave up and concentrated on freeing himself. Perhaps it would come if he worked at something else.

Unfortunately, down in the cellar, time was an illusion as there was nothing to mark its passing. He knew the chair was ready to break, but bided his time. A dull dawn light was coming in through the grimy window set at ground level. He would wait until his capturer had been and gone and then he would break free and escape through the window and be well away while he was at work.

No one came that morning. Luke didn't know how long to wait. The light didn't get much brighter, but then it was February and the days were dull.

Eventually he took a deep breath. It was now or never he decided, and with extra exertion he smashed the chair into pieces. It was not as easy disentangling himself as he had hoped, but he managed to free enough of his limbs to be able to function. He looked like he was wearing splints but was able to hobble to the window. The glass was old and thin, and he smashed through with a chair arm strapped to his own. Using shards of the glass he worked at his bonds until he managed to free his legs and the rope around his wrists. He smashed out the rest of the glass so that he didn't cut himself on his way out, throwing the pieces of chair on the floor behind him. His clothing was unconventional, but he didn't care anymore. He was free and just needed to find his way to the nearest police station. He just wished he didn't feel so dizzy and cold.

Despite hearing nothing that should worry me on the news, I am convinced I have made a mistake somewhere along the line and the police will find something to pin on me. Mother always said I would never amount to anything. I try so hard.

I cannot bear the thought of her condemnation, so I have come straight to my special place to wait for my friends. They will rally round and support me. I shall prepare a meal for them, the one I should have made the other night. The act of chopping and dicing will help to soothe me. I shall have to throw out the original ingredients because they were bought a few days ago. It's a good job I managed to pick up some fresh on my way home.

I've not even had time to see Jophiel today. It might give him time to think about his behaviour towards me. But then again he may think I have lost my feelings for him. I'll have to placate him as well. I'll just reassure him before I start the meal.

'Lisa? It's Dad.' That was unusual in itself. Her mum usually rang and never after six in the evening. She was taking the business with Luke very hard, and Lisa's first thought was that it had taken its toll and she had fallen ill.

'What's up? Is it Mum?' She felt herself start to shake. It was all getting to be too much.

'No. Well, she's in shock. But – Lees – they've found Luke.' Lisa landed with a thump on to the settee. She had so many questions, but her voice seemed to have deserted her. 'Come round, Lisa. The police are here.' He didn't sound overjoyed and she was terrified of finding out the truth.

'Is he alright?'

'Just come round. The police will tell you everything.' He put the phone down.

Lisa managed to arrive at her parents' without having or causing an accident. It was just as well they didn't live too far away. She was shaking as she tried to put her key in the lock, and a young lady in uniform let her in before heading for the kitchen.

'Come in.' It was the Detective Inspector chappie who invited her into the front room as if he owned the place. The young uniform came in and put a cup of tea on the coffee table, and indicated that she sit. Lottie was sitting on the settee beside her mother, who was crying, so Lisa sat on the other side of her and put her arm behind her, clutching at her sister's hand as she did so. She didn't trust herself to speak so stared at the Detective Inspector willing him to make things clear.

'Your brother was found alive and with non-life-threatening injuries at approximately fourteen-thirty this afternoon.' Lisa involuntarily looked at her watch. Seven forty-eight in the evening. Or nineteen forty-eight in police speak.

'We were informed at eighteen thirty-six,' he added as if by way of explanation for the delay in telling them. 'He was found on the by-pass by a passing cyclist, who called for the ambulance.' Mrs Martin let out a sob. 'He was unusually dressed and suffering from hypothermia and dehydration. The hospital made little sense of anything he was saying and felt that it was their duty to inform us. Due to the ongoing investigation we were able to ascertain his identity, which he was able to confirm.'

'What happened to him?' Lisa asked.

'As yet we cannot say. The hospital insists that further questioning is put off until tomorrow at the earliest so that they can stabilise him. He keeps lapsing in and out of consciousness. In the meantime, I have a few questions I really have to ask.'

'If it helps Luke,' Mr Martin told him.

167

The detective turned to Lisa. 'Does your brother use recreational drugs?'

'No,' she shot back rather sharply, but then thought better of it. She realised it could harm his recovery if she kept information back. 'Well, a little weed now and again.' She didn't like to look at her mum or dad, who were still living in the twentieth century.

'Nothing stronger?'

'No. I am telling you the truth. I am not aware of him taking anything other than cannabis occasionally. He likes a drink but nothing else.'

'You have stated that you and your brother don't talk much. That you have your own lives. Can you be sure?' He made it sound as if they had nothing to do with each other when they were just busy with their own lives and not interfering with each other.

Lisa hesitated. She couldn't be sure, but she knew he didn't hold with being out of control. 'I don't suppose I can, but I know Luke and I know he doesn't like the way people go over the top with alcohol or drugs. He plays rugby for the local team. He likes to stay fit.'

He didn't look as if he believed her but continued, 'Luke has a girlfriend.'

'Yes?' Lisa couldn't help but query this. 'What has Emily to do with anything?'

'You have no reason to think that he is gay?'

Mrs Martin buried her head in an already sodden handkerchief. 'What on earth gives you...? What's happened to him?' Lisa was suddenly very scared.

'We're following all avenues.' He looked towards Mrs Martin as he said this.

'I'm going to get a glass of water,' Lisa stated in a tone

that brooked no argument. The young police officer went to get up at the same time she did. 'I'll get it!' Lisa snapped looking at the Detective Inspector. Her mum had heard enough for now.

He must have understood as he followed her to the kitchen. 'Well?' she said.

'Do you want it straight?' he asked softly.

'It will come out eventually. I might as well come to terms with it here.'

He didn't pull any punches away from the parents. 'He has been drugged, beaten, tied up and sodomised. Judging by the bruising the hospital feels that it might have been against his will. He's not into such games, I take it?'

'No.'

'Only, he was wearing some rather interesting garments.'

'No. I told you.' She didn't like the way he said "garments".

'Not something you'd tell your sister.'

'I suppose not, but I'd know if he was gay at least.' He acknowledged that. 'So, what about the idea that he robbed his firm and ran away with Anni? Anneli Walsh?' Lisa was determined to set him on the right path.

'Our investigations are still ongoing.'

'But it doesn't look very promising, does it?' she pushed.

'We do have other avenues to follow.'

'Good. Are we allowed to visit him?'

'Relatives only. So, yes.'

'If you've finished, I think we'd like to go to the hospital.' He followed her into the front room.

'The family are going to the hospital,' he told his

colleague. He turned to them. 'The police are in attendance on his ward. In case he has something to tell us. We've not arrested him.' Lisa felt he'd missed off the "yet".

He's gone! Jophiel has broken his bonds and disappeared. I am stunned. He can't be far. He will have no coat and it's freezing out. Snow is forecast. He must be hiding inside. I thought he was beginning to have feelings for me. He didn't fight me last night. He might be playing. He must be playing with me. His idea of a little joke.

I've been so careful. There is nothing that could be broken or sharp. How has he done this? Where is the chair? He can't be hopping around tied to the chair?

I thought it was cold in here. He's broken the window. There's the chair. I can see the pieces of the chair all over the floor under the window. He must have battered it to pieces and used it to break the window. I'm surprised Mother didn't hear him. She never said anything when I got home. Mind you, she's still upset about the police. She's sulking and hardly speaking to me anyway.

What do I do? Look for him or attend to the female? I don't know when he did this. I didn't even see him this morning. There's dried blood on the rope and window sill. He could have gone last night for all I know. I can't be away long, or I'll arouse suspicion in Mother. I'll see if I can see a trail. If I do, I'll follow that. If I don't, I'll attend to the female and hope that he limps back for warmth. He can't know where he is. I will be his only hope if he doesn't want to freeze to death.

February 22nd

It had been a shock to see Luke the night before. He was a mess. The doctor said he'd be alright, that his injuries weren't as bad as they looked. He was malnourished, dehydrated, hypothermic and traumatised, but he'd survive. The family left him to sleep and returned in the morning. DI Clarke was already there and asked if he could see them down at the police station as soon as possible. Lisa told him it would be her as her mum and dad had had enough for the time being. She wanted to get things as straight as she could before they were told any more gruesome details. He acknowledged this and left.

She didn't stay long, feeling that two visitors were enough. Lottie was acting as go-between and hot drinks supplier while her parents kept vigil by the bedside. Luke was asleep anyway, which was probably for the best. She made her way to the police station and asked for Clarke. He must have been waiting as he appeared almost as soon as he was asked for. He took her to an interview room.

'I'm sorry. It's the only place free.' His manner was more deferential, and she took it he was beginning to come around to her way of thinking. He had one of those big brown paper bags with him. His hand was resting on it, and he kept fingering it as if he was not sure whether he should mention it or not.

A young plain-clothed lad came in with a tray and put it down on the scuffed table between them. He looked like he should still be at school and made her feel old. The tray held two cups of tea and a plate of plain biscuits.

As the door shut, Clarke cleared his throat. He pushed one of the cups towards Lisa and indicated the bag. 'This contains the clothing Luke was wearing when we picked him up.' She looked at him waiting for him to expand on the comment. He cleared his throat again. 'I would like to know if you recognise anything.' He obviously meant the "interesting garments". She suspected this would be difficult.

She picked up the tea and hugged the cup, but it was lukewarm at best. Clarke lifted the bag and tipped out the clothing. A puddle of black leather straps flowed across the table. Lisa stared, first at it and then at him. Clarke said nothing. He seemed to find his tea very interesting, but she was aware he had her in his peripheral vision. Gauging the reaction.

'He was wearing this?' Lisa stopped and tried again. 'That makes me sound like a prude. I'm not, and Luke's open-minded, but this is not something he's into,' she told Clarke. 'And don't say, "Can you be sure?" I am sure. Speak to his friends. Actually, I suppose you should be talking to Emily.' Lisa folded her arms across her chest in a defiant stance. As if she would hide anything that would help her brother. She goggled at the clothing and went to prod at it with her finger, but he stopped her.

'It's got spikes, take care.'

Using his pen Clarke shuffled it all back into the bag. 'Well, it will be tested. Vigorously. And we are speaking to his friends. And his girlfriend.'

As Lisa left, Emily came in. Clarke stood by to see if they spoke, but they had nothing much to say.

'Do you want me to wait for you?' Lisa asked and Emily nodded. 'Okay. We'll go to the hospital together if you like.'

'Thanks,' Emily whispered before disappearing into

the corridor with Clarke. As Lisa sat and waited, she considered what she had seen. What must that passer-by have thought? How many people had passed him by thinking he was a drunken pervert? Folk always jumped to the worst possible conclusion before considering the facts.

Emily was asked the same questions and shown the same "garments". There was no word on Kaz, and Luke was still asleep. Lisa doubted she would sleep again.

The female is being processed and I have called in sick in order to have time to complete the task. It will take a number of hours and I want her to be perfect as a gift for Mother. I should be able to introduce them tomorrow. I do hope they will get on. It will help me awfully if they do. I dare say there will be comments after I was seen bundling her into my car. I can ride that one out. I can say she is a cousin or something. The message I made her send to her friend will make out she left me and went home. The police will think she was picked up on her way there.

Jophiel is my main concern. He hasn't returned and I'm afraid to go looking for him for too long. Mother is suspicious enough as it is. I've heard nothing on the news about anyone being found, but then I've been so busy with the girl, and Mother would start asking her ridiculous questions if I suddenly took too much interest in what was in the news. Jophiel wouldn't know where he was as he was much disorientated. Someone must have seen him as we're hardly in the middle of nowhere here. Then again people are so self-absorbed. They might think him drunk and pass by on the other side. Perhaps he's lying frozen somewhere. I haven't said anything to my friends as yet. They don't know.

They will be so sorry for me. I spend many hours attending to their comfort and the comfort of Mother, but no one seems to have time for me. Mother is right. The world would be a better place without me. If anything has happened to Jophiel, I might just do her a favour and take her at her word. Let's see how she copes without me.

February 23rd

Lisa knew that word would fly around the hospital so chose to take compassionate leave when she realised that she didn't want to cope with the remarks, both snide and solicitous. She couldn't turn real life off like she did with social media. She crawled out of bed late the next morning, and as soon as she'd had breakfast – well – a mug of tea, half of which she tipped cold down the sink, she headed for the hospital. Their father was already there.

'They won't let us in at the moment.' Lisa hadn't realised how old he had become; colourless and tired.

'Where's Mum?' She presumed the nurses were tending to her brother and was not prepared for the next revelation.

'Luke was very distressed when he woke this morning. I think he'd been dreaming. The police are with him now.'

'Police?'

'They want a statement. The doctor isn't very happy, but I suppose the sooner we get some answers the sooner we get the person who did this. It's already been over 24 hours. Your mother's resting at home, by the way. This has taken it out of her and then some.'

'Do you want me to go home?'

'No. I want you here. You seem to be the best one when it comes to talking to the police. I didn't know what to say.' He sounded so defeated. 'Lottie's with your mum. She's going to stay for a couple more days.'

It was DI Clarke who had insisted on interrogating Luke. Lisa was about to have her say as he left the room, but he looked as tired as any of them.

Mr Martin slipped by and into Luke's room. 'Well?' Lisa stood in the Inspector's way. He flipped his notebook shut and looked towards her. A slight smile began but he stopped it and turned a professional face towards her.

'Can we talk?' He eye-pointed towards the exit. It was still very cold outside, and they ended up in a huddle in the corner of the café. 'Your brother says he was drugged and kidnapped, then kept tied in some sort of basement or cellar.' He paused and she opened her mouth to speak but he stopped her. 'He can't properly identify his kidnapper as he – or even she – was wearing a mask and wig. He was full of a drug …' He held up his hands as Lisa opened her mouth to speak. 'I'm not going to put ideas in your head.' He carried on, 'He had a particular drug in his system when his blood was tested on arrival which may alter his perceptions according to the doctor. What I want to know is – could what he says be true?'

'You're asking me?'

'I know you said he only smoked a little weed and wouldn't wear that sort of get-up, but this is between you and me. Does he do heavier drugs? Could he be having a bad trip? Would he have made this up?'

'No, no and no. You had better treat this seriously or I shall be taking it further. I …'

'It will all be investigated thoroughly, never fear. I have no intention of leaving anything to chance. On top of police professionalism …' He had a cute little smile. '… your brother thinks he recognised his assailant's mannerisms and is pointing the finger at Finnian. There is the link with Anneli Walsh. Finnian would have seen Mrs Walsh in the office. He also had access to the money.' He took a sip of his coffee. 'And your friend Katherine was last seen with him.'

Lisa suddenly felt sick and pushed her cup away. The swirl of chocolate made her giddy and just for a minute she lost focus. He lightly tapped the table next to her hand to regain her attention. 'We'll do all we can,' he assured her. Lisa just nodded glumly.

The police have been here again antagonising Mother. I had thought of making a complaint, but of course there is the link to Anneli Walsh, Luke and apparently the young lady of the night I was seen with after work. Only, she was not a lady of easy virtue but a friend of Mrs Walsh and Luke. I have a name for her too: Katherine Bailey. I decided to be gracious. I asked about Luke in the capacity of a concerned friend. I suppose he is the closest I have to a friend at the office. I also found out that he has been found, the day before yesterday, but there's been very little on the news. It only made the local and I rarely watch that. They wouldn't tell me anything. It won't look as if he stole the money and ran away with Mrs Walsh after all.

I don't suppose Mother will be speaking to me again tonight as I've brought trouble to her door. Is that such a bad thing? She doesn't like it when nothing happens and then moans when something does. She only complains about everything I try to do for her. Nothing is ever right. We'll see what she makes of her new companion. She's nearly ready. I just need to make sure her dress is suitable for her position and that her make-up is discreetly applied. Mother doesn't like make-up, but I feel that Katherine will look a little pasty without.

I am ambivalent about introducing them. Mother is never satisfied, and I don't know what I will do with Katherine if she refuses to have anything to do with her. She's so different from the rest of my friends and I cannot have the table unbalanced.

Lisa made her own way home from the hospital and locked the door. Emily stayed at Luke's bedside while Mr and Mrs Martin went home to an assortment of well-meaning neighbours. Lottie went back to her own family after visiting her brother. The police had not found any trace of Kaz, although Lisa knew they were on their way to Jonah Finnian's house. She just had to wait it out. She didn't know whether to have a drink or not. What if she had to go out again? She pushed all thoughts of identifying bodies from her mind. It was not easy. She settled for a hot chocolate with the merest dash of coffee cream liquor, but then decided what-the-hell and added a generous dollop. She could not face the noise from the television and the lights were too bright so sat in the dark nursing her cup of chocolate, listening to the creaks and ticks around her before falling asleep in the armchair.

Everything has gone wrong. I don't know what to do, which way to turn. Mother had the screaming habdabs when I introduced Katherine to her. I thought she was going to have a heart attack – which would have solved everything but, no, once she caught her breath, she threatened to call the police. She called me all sorts of vile names and went to attack me with a poker. What could I do? I had to make sure she did not. Now I've got another mess to clear up.

On top of that I need to explain my break-up with Jophiel to my friends. What will they think of me? They were so happy that I found my own special person. I will have to explain that I was wrong. It will be like Mother all over again. They will see me for the failure I am, and I will be less than worthless in their eyes.

I can't stay at Mother's. I can't face my friends and work is unbearable. Where can I go?

February 23rd (evening)

Lisa woke to the buzz of the doorbell and was barely alert as she opened it. 'Harry?' After all this, here he was standing on the doorstep.

'I need to explain.' He looked contrite. 'Will you invite me in?' Lisa was speechless. Did he know anything about what she had been going through? Did he think he could just turn up, out of the blue, and carry on as if nothing had happened? Now that it looked as if the police investigation had taken the right turn, she could see more clearly what a mug Harry had taken her for. She wanted to say, 'Fuck off!' and slam the door in his face. On the other hand, she also wanted to hear what sorry excuse he had come up with while she had been struggling on her own. Lisa was beyond angry and was ready to make him suffer. She opened the door just wide enough to allow him through and stood back without speaking. Head down, he made his way towards the living area. This was going to be interesting.

'Well?' Lisa stood with her arms folded across her chest. She did not invite him to sit.

He lifted his head and looked her in the eye. 'I have something to tell you,' he began. 'Something I have wanted to tell you for a long time but …' He paused, took a deep breath, and carried on. She didn't interrupt; she wanted him to hang himself. '… I thought – because our relationship was so new I couldn't bring myself to.'

'It had better be good.' She stared right back.

He swallowed. 'I've not been strictly truthful with you…'

'I found that out for myself,' she snapped.

He flinched but carried on. 'I don't work at the hospital. I sort of gate-crashed the Christmas dinner.'

'I know that too. How do you think I felt when I was told? Everybody was listening when Glenda came downstairs to tell me you didn't exist as far as the hospital was concerned. I felt such a fool.' She was on the verge of tears. Tears of frustration, she was not going to shed real tears over him!

'I've not been well …'

'What do you want? An "I've been a brave boy sticker"?' she retorted. He flinched again.

'I'm HIV positive.' He said no more. Just looked her in the eye for a second before turning away. That little disclosure took the wind out of her sails. Lisa's first uncharitable thought was, "What shady activity has he been up to to get that?" Fortunately, she didn't say anything as he carried on.

'My mother was attacked and raped when I was a baby.' She made to interrupt, but he stopped her by raising his hand. 'Let me tell it before I lose the courage.' Lisa nodded and indicated he sat. He ignored her and took a deep breath. 'She didn't tell anyone at first. Not for a long time in fact. She was embarrassed and afraid. I mean, everyone knew she slept around. She didn't even know who my father was. She felt it was her fault and pretended it hadn't happened but unfortunately, she contracted HIV. She passed it to me as she was still feeding me at the time. Once she realised what had happened, she attempted suicide. She died after the third attempt. I was three years old, and I have paid the price.'

Lisa's legs felt suddenly weak and she sat heavily on the settee. She didn't know what to say, so asked, 'Where have you been?' She needed to know, needed to know if the ordeal had left him a monster. She didn't want to think that he had anything to do with Luke's nightmare or Kaz's disappearance, because that would mean she had helped him, however inadvertently.

'Unfortunately, the delay in treatment has left me with some problems.'

'Where have you been for the past week?' Lisa insisted. She was determined he would not sway her with a sympathy vote.

'Hospital for more tests. For some of the time. Then thinking.'

'Do you know my brother?' Lisa wasn't expecting the truth.

'Yes.' Such a simple answer it threw her. 'I have a court case pending. Compensation for an accident I was in – I'm not in any trouble.'

Lisa ignored the latter comment. 'Were you trying to get to him through me?'

'No. I was trying to get to you through him.'

Her mouth formed the word 'Oh' but she made no sound.

'I have come to offer you an explanation, my sincerest apologies and say goodbye. I owe you that.'

He had lied and let her down. She was angry and hurt through his actions, but although she had intended to finish the relationship, she suddenly didn't want it to end. Not like this anyway.

'Stay. I'll put the kettle on. Tell me everything.'

I don't know what to do. I try to leave by the front door, but the police are already here. I turn and head for the back door, but there are uniforms there as well. Mother is still here on the floor. One look at her and I'll have some explaining to do.

The police are battering down the door. I've left the hall light on. They know I'm here. They can see me through the glass.

I head for the cellar. My friends will help me. I can say I was with them all the while and Mother must have been mugged by an intruder. They will back me up. It's a good job I have fitted bolts on the inside of the door. It was to stop Mother prying while I was entertaining, but they will stop the police now.

It's still such a mess down here. I've not mended the window properly, nor have I cleared everything away after

processing Katherine. I was so excited about presenting her
to Mother – to make her proud of me. I can't do it now, I'm
too upset. I'll go next door and meet my friends. They'll be
arriving soon expecting supper. In fact, I can hear someone
in there already. What am I to tell them? I don't ...

'Jonah Finnian?'

February 23rd (late evening)

'Have you anyone to stay with you?' Lisa didn't answer.
'Someone you could go to?'

'Well, it would have been Kaz.' She could hardly say
her name. She couldn't believe she was dead. Vibrant, silly
Kaz, her bestie since high school. The tears came
unbidden; she couldn't stop them so turned back to
making tea. DI Clarke waited. He must have dealt with
grieving people before. The uniform took the mugs from
her shaking hands and set them down on the coffee table.
And she wasn't the only one he would have to deal with.
There were seven families who would now have closure.
Seven families grieving for their dead. Seven families who
would have to hear the gruesome details of how their
loved ones died and what had happened to them after
death. That was the stuff of nightmares.

It would be all over the papers and on the news. Lisa
wouldn't be able to get away from it. Fortunately, she was
still not in work. She couldn't face the gossip and the pity
there. Perhaps when something else happened and
became the main topic of conversation she'd try a few
hours. The hospital had been very good about that.

They are calling me Hannibal Lecter. How ridiculous. I wouldn't eat my friends. When it says I had them for meals it doesn't mean that literally. I cooked the most delicious food for them. I enjoyed their company. I took away their stupid, dull, urban names and gave them ones that lifted the soul and helped them to soar. I made them into something they could never be living on the streets of this godforsaken town. If I had been named after an angel like my uncles, I would have made something of myself. Instead I was a Jonah, bringer of bad luck. I was giving them the chance I never had.

I know now that my mistake was in inviting the women. Women are always trouble. Look at Mother. She told me that as I grew up. 'Keep away from girls,' she said. 'Otherwise you'll bring trouble on this house.' She was right. I shouldn't have taken the girls. The men, the street boys who relished my company, were not missed enough to be reported, but I messed up with the women. I just wanted everything to balance, like in the films Mother watches. An Eve for every Adam. If she'd have just let me be me, everything would have been alright. Life is diverse – not that she understood that.

March

In the end Lisa rang Harry and invited him over. He had finally given her a number where she could reach him. They had a long talk and decided to remain friends. He was much more relaxed, and human, since he had confided in her, although he was still reticent compared to many of the young men she knew. Probably his mother's influence. He had been carrying his secrets for a very long time. Also, she felt she needed someone not so emotionally involved as family. Lisa needed someone to trust, and although it might seem ridiculous to others, she knew she could trust him not to push himself or his thoughts forward, and he proved a reliable sounding board. She also knew he would like things to go further, but she was hesitant. Besides she and DI Clarke, Ian, were sort of dating. It was early days and the case had not yet gone to court, but they got on well enough.

'I've seen the papers.' Harry looked at her. 'How are you coping?' Lisa couldn't answer as she wasn't sure she was. 'Stupid question?' She nodded. 'I can go if you want?'

Strangely she didn't want him to go. 'No. I asked you here.'

The papers and news channels were full of pictures of the cellar under Jonah Finnian's house. They showed his makeshift laboratory where he carried out his work, the grisly tools, and carboys half full of chemicals. They also showed a tastefully furnished room with a dining table, set ready for eight people; perfectly arranged with expensive china, shining silver cutlery and sparkling crystal.

Only the exquisitely preserved bodies had been removed.

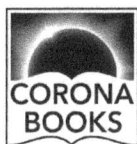

Independent Publishers of the
Best in New Genre Short Fiction (and More)

Corona Books UK was established in 2015. Our primary focus is on publishing the best new short stories in horror, sci-fi and speculative fiction.

For the latest on other titles published by us and forthcoming attractions, please visit our website and follow us on X.

www.coronabooks.com

@CoronaBooksUK

Readers of this book may also be interested in checking out *The Corona Book of Horror Stories* book series (4 volumes), *The Corona Book of Ghost Stories* and *The Corona Book of Science Fiction*, all of which include stories by Sue Eaton, amongst many other great short stories.

www.ingramcontent.com/pod-product-compliance
Ingram Content Group UK Ltd.
Pitfield, Milton Keynes, MK11 3LW, UK
UKHW042219270725
461263UK00002B/35

9 781999 657970